ASTRAY

A Tale of Time Travel, Love, and Indecency

ANTHONY LERRO

This is a work of fiction. The characters, incidents, and dialogue are from the author's imagination. Any resemblance to actual events or persons, living or dead, is entirely coincidental.

ASTRAY

A Tale of Time Travel, Love, and Indecency

ISBN 979-8-9924539-0-4

Cover by Andrea Saldutti

To my sister, for always being my biggest supporter.

Contents

Preface And Acknowledgments

In March of 2017, I was an accounting major in my junior year of college. I had become interested in the filmmaking process and my critical opinion on film and television seemed to be ever growing. So, to test myself I decided to see if I could write a screenplay.

After a handful of months of failing to complete a first draft of an initial story idea, I then decided to sit down and write a sci-fi dystopian thriller that had been brewing in my mind for months, and in September fresh on my senior year I had produced a feature length script. At the time I had thought I had written the next *Blade Runner*. Now I can look back and laugh with honesty and humility because it really was not that great and should never see the light of the day. However, it did show me that I could do it. I could sit down and have the patience and fortitude to write the vision that I had in my head from start to finish.

Excited and proud of my accomplishment, I immediately started thinking about what movie idea I was going to write next. About a week later I was driving in the car listening to *Nature Boy* by Nat King Cole. Now if you're wondering what college student listens to Nat King Cole, I can honestly say I don't remember why. I should have been listening to Avicii, Kygo, or whatever EDM artist or song that I normally would have been blasting in the car. But as the lyrics of the song started, I immediately imagined a man in his late twenties, twenty-eight would be the specific age I would choose days later, coincidently the same age I am now as I publish this novella. I immediately imagined this character walking through the 1950s after he had time traveled with *Nature Boy* playing in the background, which in this work is the opening of chapter four.

Over the next week I started asking myself all the necessary questions. Who is this guy? How did he get there? How is he going to get back to the future? I quickly knew the story was going to have mobsters, a romance at the center, a 1950s soundtrack to which some of the songs are mentioned in this work. And I even knew what the very last scene was going to be. After daydreaming for a week, I finally got to writing.

The first draft of the script had a hurdle. As someone who at the time refused to outline, I quickly was able to crank out what was about the first thirty pages but then got stuck at the first scene that required some exposition, which in this work is chapter six. I hadn't worked out the details that were required in that scene. So, for a month I just kept sprucing up the first thirty pages while I went back to daydreaming of a potential solution. In that month no answer arrived and then came the realization that I was stuck and should put down the script, and maybe one day I would figure it out.

Two weeks before graduation I was in the gym when the answer just hit me out of nowhere. I quickly wrote down the idea on my phone, and by the end of June 2018 I had completed the first draft of the screenplay.

In an earlier attempt at writing this preface I expanded upon my own journey of writing and trying to navigate through the film industry or lack there off. Briefly I will just say that in 2022 I had made the commitment to try and get Astray made and seek independent financing. After a year and half of exhausting every resource I had or could think of, and continued frustration with nobody giving me the time of day, I decided to get this story out there in the form of a book, as writing a novelization of the film was always an idea that I had. I just assumed it would come after the film was released.

Turning this script into a novella was the reverse engineered way of how these things usually happen. Adapting the screenplay into a book gave me new and exciting ways to expand upon the story and the characters that I initially was unable to do. The silver lining of it all is that through this process I was able to make improvements, and if I had gotten the financing to make the movie, these improvements would not exist, and that version of the film would certainly not be as good as the potential version I hope I get a chance to make someday.

With writing this book comes great risk. If the response is negative, then certainly a film version would not be attractive to any potential producers or investors. But risks need to be taken and so I throw this story out into the world.

Now I will take this time to give out some acknowledgments. First, I want to thank my alpha and beta readers. Thank you to Connor, Matt, Andrea A., and my sister. Especially grateful to the latter two who both read very early drafts of the screenplay back in 2018 and 2019.

I want to thank Andrea S. for his amazing artwork and his patience and ability to take my vision for the cover, which is what I had always seen as the movie poster, and make it come alive with great suggestions and improvements. Back in 2022 he and I storyboarded out the opening scene which you will soon read in the first chapter. Maybe in the near future I will show off some of those panels on social media. His work on those is incredible.

I also want to thank my editor Morgan Macedo at Glasswing Editing for her diligent work.

I want to thank all my friends and family for their support, especially my sister and parents.

Lastly, I will say I'm very proud of this book. I'm excited to share it and quite eager and curious to see what the reaction is going to be. This story has been with me for over seven years. Michael, Clara, Frankie, and the rest of the gang have lived inside my head all that time. Make no mistake, my goal someday is still to turn this into a film. I hope this story and characters are well received and people enjoy it. Who knows, maybe one day this novella will find its way into the hands of the right person.

Chapter 1

The Shootout

The fall couldn't have been more than three feet, but hitting the side of your face on asphalt does not tickle. Michael frantically gasped for air as he pushed himself up on his hands and knees, never losing grip of the Glock in his right hand.

A car coming down the road slammed on its brakes. The driver quickly exited the vehicle. "What in the... Are you all right?"

Michael paid the man no attention as he looked at his surroundings. The summer morning sun was pounding down on the road with no clouds in sight. The homes with their perfectly cut green lawns, and the cars, specifically the one idling nearly two feet from him, looked as if they were from the 1950s or '60s. If only he was into cars as much as some of his friends, he probably could have pinpointed the year of the Ford that was breathing on him. It did not pair well with the heat radiating off the black road he'd been intimately introduced to.

He knew what had happened but was still in disbelief. And, quite honestly, getting the air to recirculate in his lungs was more of a focus at the given moment.

"Here, let me help you up," said the driver. Without permission, he hoisted Michael up, who was dressed in black slacks, and a navy button-down shirt that had sweat bleeding through it.

Then three noises—thuds just like the one Michael had made when he hit the road face-first—came from behind the car. His heart started beating even quicker.

He peaked his head around the man and saw his three pursuers with their pistols at the ready. Before he could even think, three blasts rang out. Michael ducked behind the car as fast as he could. Falling with him was the driver, who had three bullet wounds piercing his back. With no time to help the kind man, Michael got up and ran for cover.

He sprinted through a nearby yard as bullets zipped past him. The adrenaline pumping made him feel superhuman. He reached the end of the yard and took cover on the side of the house, returning fire at the three men chasing him. One took a bullet in the chest and crumpled to the ground. Another took cover behind a tree, while the other went to the opposite side of the house.

A round went off from behind the tree, and Michael dipped back behind the wall before quickly returning fire. He hit the man in the forehead, sending the assailant's head to pull backward, taking the rest of his body with him.

Michael cautiously peaked around the corner but did not see his final attacker. He then moved down the side of the house toward the backyard with his gun at the ready. As he reached the edge, he met his last assailant. They grappled before both hitting the ground, losing their guns in the fall.

The man had Michael pinned, and he quickly moved his hands around Michael's throat. As the man choked him, Michael got his right leg onto the man's chest and kicked him off, sending him staggering and landing on his backside.

Michael turned and saw his gun on the ground behind him. He crawled for it as fast as he could, and in one fluent motion, he grabbed it, turned, and fired three bullets that tore into the man's chest.

Breathing heavily, Michael got up and wiped the sweat from his eyes. Before the sigh of relief could hit, police sirens roared in the distance. Michael immediately ran for the fence in the backyard and climbed over out of sight.

Chapter 2
The Day Before

Happy birthday!—a phrase that lost excitement after the 21st occasion. And here on the 28th festivity for Michael Morrano, just two years away from three decades of existence, the magic showed no signs of returning.

The day started off like any other in Michael's South Philadelphia one-bedroom apartment, except for the birthday wishes blowing up his phone from family and friends and the mental preparation for the dinner celebration at his mother's house later, interrogation is the term he would use.

He ate leftover Chinese takeout for breakfast, worked out, ate again, and screwed around on YouTube for large chunks at a time. A nap always made its way in there somewhere, usually after his self-love time.

He arrived at his mother's house in his navy button-down shirt and black slacks. The ensemble was finished off with his badge and gun. His outfit seemed to draw criticism from the peanut gallery, which consisted of his mother Angela, sister Mary, and his grandmother.

Navy doesn't go with black.

What's with the dark colors? You trying to be in the mafia?

He needs a wardrobe change.

The criticisms of the Italian American female arbiters of taste seemed to have no end. He thought the colors went well with his dark hair and eyes, aided by his tan skin, fresh off a weekend at the Jersey Shore.

Dinner went as expected. The interrogation ensued on why he was still single, the importance of getting married and having kids, and the preference of getting married to an Italian girl was not missed by his grandmother. He was into

Italian chicks, but he always joked with himself that that was just what he needed—another Italian woman in his life to give him attitude. His previous and only serious girlfriend had been Italian. Michael had been no saint in the relationship, but after two years with a consistently unhappy partner, hearing "do what you want" and "you're an asshole" had been enough for him to jump ship. So, for the past year and half, he had been single with zero effort put toward the dating game, and he was happier for it. He had always wondered if the real, authentic Italian women born and bred in Italy were any easier. Probably not.

He enjoyed the pasta, cutlets, and meatballs, along with the entertainment that naturally ensued. As the marriage and kid talk regurgitated after dessert, he quickly got the hell out of there.

Michael's Ford Crown Victoria sped through the streets of Philadelphia with "Night Fever" by the Bee Gees playing through the radio. He had been a detective for almost a full year. He enjoyed his job, and working nights fed into his night-owl tendencies.

His partner, Sam, was in the passenger seat, enthusiastically singing along. He wore the same outfit as Michael, except his choice of blue was powder, not navy. He was a few years Michael's senior and shared the same type of humor, which made working with him enjoyable. He was not Italian, but he had dated some Italian girls and knew enough cultural jokes to always be ripping on Michael. Sam was of Irish descent—brown hair accompanied the red complexion of his pale skin, which the summers did not seem to help.

"Calm down, Tony Manero," said Michael as he turned down the radio.

"Tony Manero was a dancer, not a singer," said Sam. "Happy birthday by the way. When are we going to Hide and Seek?"

"I am not going to Hide and Seek," Michael replied definitively while keeping his eyes on the road.

"Bro, you tell me who you want, and I will make sure they give you the best lap dance you've ever had. Seriously full-contact European style. I've got the in with Chloe, Sugar, Harley, Raven, Luna... You pick bro."

"Hide and Seek is where all the eighteen-year-olds go." A true statement, as that's where half of Michael's senior class had gone after turning eighteen.

"What do you want to go to Winny's with the forty-year-olds? And where are the meatballs? I know Angela made plenty."

"I ate them all."

"That's bullshit. It's not an Italian meal if there aren't leftovers."

"You're not getting any after last time when you ate all the veal piccata."

"Fuck off with that. There was like only two medallions. And who just eats one veal medallion?"

"There were three!" fired back Michael, who took the robbing of some great veal personally.

"Well, they were good. What the fuck do you want me to tell you? And I gotta say, I'm fucking hungry. So if you're not coughing up any meatballs we gotta stop."

⚫

Less than an hour later, the two of them were wolfing down cheesesteaks on a bench. It was their goal to try every cheesesteak joint they could find in the city and be the food critics they thought they were. They debated amongst themselves about what cheese was preferred and how many onions were too many onions. Sometimes they got pizza or burgers, and they would joke about starting their own YouTube channel or social media account where they would review all the foods that made working out a necessity. Of course, the whole point of the idea was reviewing food on the job as detectives and having a clever title. They'd settled upon "Dining Detectives" and made a test video on Michael's phone. Their superiors were not thrilled with the endeavor. They showed their sergeant the video, and his response was not what you would call encouraging.

"So did they give you the whole marriage bullshit?" asked Sam as they finished up their last bites.

"Does a bear shit in the woods?" answered Michael with emphatic sarcasm.

"Jesus Christ. I mean, why would you want that when you got me, huh? You're practically married to me anyway."

"I tell them when the right one comes, I'll know, and I'll try not to fuck up."

The two of them rolled up their trash and looked around, taking in the quiet hours of the city. "God we're fucking dead tonight," said Sam.

Michael leaned back against the bench with a sigh, and Sam looked over at his partner. "What?"

Michael unenthusiastically gave the response his partner was hoping to hear. "Hide and Seek?"

Sam smiled.

———◄O►———

Michael had been to a strip club once before. He could not say he didn't enjoy the experience, but seeing a topless chick in her 20s with a man who looked like he was one missed dialysis treatment away from dying made him feel scummy.

The experience at Hide and Seek did not disappoint. Sam even set up a birthday shoutout from the DJ, and right on cue, Luna took Michael upstairs into a private room where she laid out the rules for a European-style lap dance, wishing him a happy birthday before she performed her act.

They left the club around one in the morning with their ears ringing and their wallets lighter. "How was Luna? Best birthday present ever?" asked Sam with a sly grin, expecting to know the answer. Michael just laughed to himself.

As thoughts of Luna and the night danced in his head—figuratively and literally—they were abruptly cut off by the sound of a man screaming for help.

Their attention was grabbed by the noise, and they caught the sight of a man's legs being dragged into an alley and out of sight.

Michael and Sam looked at each other, disappointed their duties weren't finished. But their willingness and better judgment steered them to break up whatever nonsense was happening before heading home.

As they approached the scene, Michael stepped on something that did not sound or feel like concrete. He looked down and saw a map. He picked it up and unfolded it, revealing a red circle on a location he did not recognize far west beyond the city.

Before Michael could turn around, a cloth came up over his face, and the dream took him.

———— ◄O► ————

Michael was back inside the strip club. The place was empty, and he was sitting in a chair on the stage.

A topless Luna came out from around the corner and strutted over to Michael. She sat on his lap and leaned in, burying his face between her breasts.

He wished the dream did not end so soon.

Chapter 3
<u>The Window</u>

M ichael awoke in the back of an SUV. His legs were being pulled, then his shoulders were being hoisted up. Sam, the man they'd been trying to rescue in the alley, and Michael were all dragged out of the car, their hands already zip-tied. Michael, with one size up of the unknown man, assumed he was in his forties and slept with a number of different vices.

They were walked over to a barn. Michael reared his head to see his two captors and glimpsed they were both well-dressed, similarly to himself, and were both well-built with dark hair. Mobsters were certainly his guess.

To the right of the barn was an old-style farmhouse, and surrounding the perimeter of the farm was a cornfield. To the left, just north of the stalks, the sun was rising amidst the chatter of birds and the soft hum of crickets.

Michael felt a little groggy or loopy—he did not know the right word to describe the feeling of waking up from whatever concoction sent him to the sandman, which was a great sleep, nonetheless.

Michael dreaded that the steps to the barn were going to be his last. There is a feeling and look that people give you when they are mad, whether you cut them off in traffic or take a dump on their porch. Then there is a look and feel when someone wants to kill you, and Michael would never forget it or mistake it again.

Michael could feel his heart racing and the adrenaline starting to dump. He had the feeling he had to pee, which could have been from the current fear or the alcohol from the night before was now looking for an exit.

In the end, it is a weird feeling when you know the reaper is at the door.

As they entered the barn, the three of them were thrown forward onto their faces. The two mobsters lifted them up on their knees. Michael looked up, and shock and awe were expressed on his face.

A shimmering abyss in the shape of a vertical rectangle was hovering off the ground in the middle of the barn. A faint white light poured out of it. It was the only thing in the barn except for a few stacks of hay and some old, rusted tools.

Michael initially wondered if this was a lasting effect of the potion that had knocked him out or if someone had spiked his drink at the bar, for logic and reason had gone out the door.

Michael looked over at Sam, who seemed to be asking himself the same question. *What in the hell?*

The third member of their trinity did not take the situation well. "Tell Giuseppe I'll pay! I swear I'll pay!" One of the mobsters' pistol-whipped him, knocking him unconscious.

"Easy! And take those badges off while you're at it. Can't let disposal know we had to grab two boys in blue," said the other mobster.

Michael now definitively knew who they were, after the third stooge said the name Giuseppe. They were mobsters for the Philadelphia crime family. It was common knowledge that the mob did not go after law enforcement or civilians, but the circumstances were what they were, and it was clear they had screwed up. The mobster who'd pistol-whipped the man grabbed both of their badges off their waists.

Michael immediately clenched his fists together with his wrists facing each other. It was a maneuver he had seen watching random videos on YouTube. Little had he known how handy it would be.

"I'll give you the cops if you let me have the squealer," said the pistol-whipping mobster.

Michael was close to getting his right thumb free.

"Let disposal figure out what they want to do. They got three, for Christ's sake."

Michael's thumb was out and subsequently his hand, keeping it concealed from his kidnappers. He exchanged a look with Sam.

"What if they ask about these two?"

"Just keep your mouth—" The mobster was suddenly taken to the ground by Sam, who'd rolled himself into him, taking out his legs.

Michael got up and went for the other mobster. But before he could reach the man, he pulled out his gun and shot Sam in the chest. The shot at close range inside the barn rang in Michael's ears as he tackled his target.

Michael saw the now loose gun and dove for it, turned, and pulled the trigger. The mobster fell but his friend was unphased, and he jumped on top of Michael, knocking the gun away. He pummeled Michael twice in the face before Michael was able to block the third attempt and rolled on top of him, exchanging positions. He could feel himself going feral as his life-or-death instincts kicked in. He mercilessly wailed on his adversary. With each punch he landed, he let out a sound of aggression he had never heard before, that slowly became more audible as the ringing in his ears died down. He connected punch after punch until the man was beat into submission.

Michael had to take some deep breaths to decompress himself, then he got up and ran over to Sam, calling out his name and hoping for some sign of life. No response or breath came as Michael checked for the nonexistent pulse.

After mutters of anger and frustration, Michael grabbed his badge, the keys to the car, and a clip for the mobster's pistol before dragging Sam's body out of the barn.

He got Sam and himself into the car and put it in drive. He sped onto the path that exited the property before an SUV pulled in front of him, blocking the way. They both slammed on the brakes, avoiding a collision, but not avoiding eye contact through the windshields. The look the SUV driver gave was not what you would call affectionate.

Michael's look was easily described by his response: "Oh shit."

He threw the car in reverse and looked through the rearview seeing the cornstalks. He pressed hard on the gas, accelerating toward his only escape route.

As he hit the stalks, the car crashed to a stop as if it had run into a giant hammer. The airbag subsequently smacked him in the face. He unbuckled his seatbelt and looked behind him to see a metal fence that discreetly walled the property. He gained his composure and rolled out of the car, forced to leave his friend's body behind.

The fence was barbed at the top, so he bolted to the barn—his only sanctuary. As he ran, he heard the opening and shutting of car doors followed by the bangs and zips of bullets flying by him.

Inside, there was nowhere to hide. He stopped in his tracks and focused on the shimmering abyss in front of him. The warmth of the white light poured out, almost like it was drawing him in.

Don't go to the light, huh?

The growing shouts of the mobsters coming for him left him with only one choice. "Fuck." Michel ran to the abyss and dove through.

Chapter 4

<u>1959</u>

M ichael stood on a street corner surveying the 1950s-style town. It was like he had been transported into a movie or some old photograph. He watched the cars and the people go by. He could only imagine what he looked like being so disheveled after the barn fight and now a shootout that had certainly disrupted the peaceful morning for the denizens of the community. Everyone seemed nicer and happier here. No one was worried about their phones or social media, which reminded him—he took out his phone and held it up, trying to get service. *Worth a try*.

After the shootout, he stealthily exited the neighborhood through a wooded area. He finally got a chance to relieve himself. His urine came out nearly as yellow as lemon-lime Gatorade, which was a visible reminder of how thirsty he was. Afterward, he stumbled upon the town, and here he was, holding some future piece of technology up in the air like the holy grail, looking for some nonexistent magical entity. He put his phone away before proceeding down the street.

The town was small, with one main street, and a few ancillary streets to it with a handful of traffic lights. Kids ran by playing with a bouncy ball, and two young ladies walking by smiled at him.

I guess I don't look that bad.

He stopped at a TV store, looking at the old dial sets. Next to it was a newspaper stand that Michael quickly helped himself to, even though he had never read a newspaper in his life. On top of the front page, the date read July

18, 1959. He shook his head and rubbed his eyes, hoping for the off chance he would wake up back in his apartment, but there he was, still in the dream. *1959.*

He looked up from the newspaper to see a diner across the street. His dehydration was setting in, mixed with what felt like a gaping hole in his stomach. It turned out getting in a long continuous fight and chase after a night of drinking doesn't serve the body well. He had not eaten since the cheesesteaks with Sam, which seemed to worsen his hunger on the spot. Sam—his partner whose body was slowly decaying back at the farm in the middle of God knows where. Michael remembered the clue on the map he'd stepped on. They must have been taken west of the city to Middle-of-Nowhere, Pennsylvania. But as sadness and frustration sat in, his hunger and thirst were overpowering.

Before he crossed the street, a cop car and ambulance flew by, which brought a simultaneous smirk and sigh.

I wonder who that is for.

—◆—

Clara Giordano walked to work, humming Bobby Darin's new song, "Dream Lover." Her walk to work was routine. She left her house at the same time every day after putting on her waitress uniform and pulling up her black hair into a ponytail, before getting yelled at by her Italian mother for not eating.

She would then make her trek out of the neighborhood and cross the bridge on the outskirts of town, passing the first of the few small waterfalls in the area, before crossing the main one at the heart of the town. Lazia Falls was a beautiful town to visit, but for Clara, it was not her ideal place to live.

During the summer, tourists would travel in and take pictures around the falls, shop at the local stores, and go hiking through the woods. Some townies did not like the tourists, but Clara knew it was financially beneficial to the town—and to herself—as more people made their way into the diner. Tourists were generally happy, and happy customers tended to tip well.

She had been waitressing at Lou's Diner since she was 16, and over the course of the past eight years, it seemed that each year went by quicker than the previous.

The morning at work started off no different than any other. She got there early and helped Lou open. The diner's booths followed along the windows around the perimeter, with a large bar stretching half the width of the interior.

Her best friend and coworker, Marissa Altamura, showed up late as always, accompanied by an excuse or an elaborate story of some supposed crazy occurrence. The opening line was always, "Clara you won't believe what just happened."

This morning's excuse was something about a bunch of cop cars speeding down the street, and so-and-so told so-and-so they'd heard gunshots, and, per usual, Clara just laughed it off.

When a few cop cars sped by minutes later, Marissa gloated, "Told ya!"

Clara and Marissa had been best friends since second grade. Marissa was bolder than Clara and always kept things interesting. Namely the time they got caught stealing lipstick when they were eleven. It had been Marissa's idea, and Clara, despite her best efforts, could not persuade her otherwise. Clara's police chief of a father had, of course, not been thrilled with the situation. Saying he'd been livid would be an understatement. But all these years later, they were still stuck in the small-town life, serving up burgers and omelets.

They were both Italian American like the near entirety of Lazia Falls that had a population just south of five thousand. It was almost like there was a sign at the outskirts that said *Italians Only*. But few ever left, and the parents made sure that the tomato-sauce bloodlines stayed pure—or gravylines, but that was a different debate entirely. They often joked how terrible Italian guys were and that the German, Irish, and Jewish immigrant pools had to be better. Their Roman Catholic parents would love the latter of the three for sure. In all honesty, they did not find Italian guys terrible, just any chance they could make fun of their Italian fathers directly or indirectly was an opportunity they could not pass up, and the well never seemed to dry up of material.

Marissa and Clara were behind the counter. Marissa was counting the money her table had just left her. She shook her head, not thrilled with the gratuity. "It's always the ones you work extra for who screw ya," she said.

The diner's door opened, and Michael walked in, immediately catching the eye of the two young waitresses. Marissa squinted as he approached Clara. "Excuse me, do I just sit anywhere or is there—"

"Anywhere you like is fine," said Clara.

"Thanks," said Michael as he gave her a tiny smirk. She returned one as he walked away, then turned her attention to Marissa, who gave Michael a doubletake.

"What?" asked Clara.

"Is that Dion DiMucci?"

"Who?" Clara looked around.

"The singer." Marissa started to sing "I Wonder Why".

"I know who Dion DiMucci is. Who are you talking about?"

Marissa pointed to Michael. "Him."

"Him? You think that's Dion?" Clara let out a laugh at the notion.

"It could be."

"He looks like Dion if he was hungover," said Clara emphatically.

"Rockstar lifestyle. Look at Elvis."

"I am telling you, that's not Dion."

"He doesn't have to be Dion to go take his order."

Clara looked over at the man in question. "He's in your section."

"If he's hungover, chances are he ain't going to tip well." Marissa ended the discussion by going to help a different table.

Clara shook her head.

As she walked over to Michael, she noticed his somber demeanor. There was dirt on his shirt and pants, along with some sweat stains. She was intrigued by him, not because she thought he was Dion or some other famous singer, but because it was clear he was not from around here, which immediately made anyone more interesting in Clara's eyes. "Hi, I'm Clara. I'll be your waitress this morning. Can I get you anything?"

Michael, returning from his head in the clouds, was taken back by the interruption. "Yeah, uh, I'll just have a coffee for now, thanks."

"Coffee it is." She walked over to the coffee station, noticing Marissa following her over. After she grabbed the pot and poured the cup, the questions ensued.

"What's his name?"

"It's not Dion."

"That doesn't mean you can't start up a conversation. You know what our parents say, Italians are supposed to marry Italians so we can make—"

"More Italian babies." Clara turned with the cup in her hand. "So that's what you want? You want me to go take him for a spin right there in the booth?" she asked with attitude. "Why don't I ask Dion just to marry me then? Let's get Father Sacripanti down here while we're at it to do to the ceremony so I don't fornicate and send my soul to burn in hell for all of eternity."

Marissa put her hands on her hips, smirking. "I thought you said he's not Dion."

Clara rolled her eyes and went to deliver the coffee.

"And it's called confession, we have it for a reason," Marissa called out to her friend.

"Here you go," said Clara as she reached his table.

"Thanks." He looked up at her and smiled, holding it for a couple seconds longer than he should have. It gave her a chance to start a conversation with the assumed tourist.

"You okay?" she asked.

"Yeah, I've just had an interesting day so far, to say the least."

"Must be some day." Clara checked the clock. "It's not even ten yet."

"Yeah, you wouldn't believe me."

"Try me?"

Michael paused for a second. He thought about blurting out the words *time travel* and seeing what response he would get. He could always just say it was joke. Nobody would believe him anyway. But his better judgment got the best of him. "What is your name again?" he asked.

"Clara. You're not from around here, are you?"

"No, not at all. That obvious?"

"It's just that this is not that large of a town. It's pretty easy to pick out the strangers."

"I'm Michael, by the way."

"Knew it."

"Excuse me?"

"Sorry, never mind." She shook her head, smiling.

"At least now you can't call me a stranger."

"Well, if you need anything else, just let me know." She smiled again and walked back to the counter where Marissa was eagerly waiting.

"What's with the smile?" asked Marissa.

Clara leaned over the counter. *This will be good.* "It's actually Dion," she whispered with a serious tone.

"No! You're kidding?" Marissa whispered back.

"No, you were right. I swear to God."

"Really?" Marissa bounced with excitement.

"I swear on the Lord."

Marissa jumped. "Oh my God, it's him. I knew it!"

"You've got to go get his autograph."

"Oh my God." Marissa sped over to his table, trying not to run. Clara laughed to herself at how gullible Marissa was. She knew that she harbored a magazine with Dion on the cover.

Marissa slowed down her walk as she approached Michael's table, and Clara tuned in to enjoy the show. "Hi, I just want to say, I'm a huge fan and I love your music and if you could like give me an autograph that would mean so much."

Michael looked up with confusion as he took a sip of his coffee. His face of bewilderment lasted a few seconds before he gave his response. "I have no clue what the hell you're talking about."

Marissa made a face of mad realization before turning around and stomping over to a laughing Clara.

"What the fuck?" Michael said to himself, taking another sip of coffee.

Before Michael could put his head back into the clouds, a napkin dropped onto the table. He lifted his head to see the man who left it exit the diner. He read the napkin. *Side alley*. He quickly got up and dropped some cash onto the table before following the man out the door.

Clara watched Michael leave, filled with disappointment.

Michael stood outside the diner's door and looked both ways, noticing the alley to his right. He proceeded to it and cautiously turned the corner to see only a dumpster. He took a few steps forward and slowly turned his head around, keeping it on a swivel.

Whack!

Michael was knocked to the ground.

As he looked up to the narrow sliver of sky above the alley, the light of the summer sun was losing to the darkness creeping in on all sides.

Not again.

In less than two seconds, it engulfed him. Not even two hours awake, the deep dreamy sleep took him again.

Chapter 5
Jackass

The church was silent. Only two souls were present inside.

The confessional's slider opened, revealing a screen only large enough to view the lower half of the soul's faces. The layman spoke before the priest. "Bless me Father for I have sinned. It's been two weeks since my last confession."

"You may confess your sins," the priest responded.

"The usual stuff—took the Lord's name in vain, missed mass, jerked off a bunch of times, and stole some shit, the usual," said the man with a nonchalant attitude. No regret was found upon any syllable he spoke.

"But are you truly sorry?" asked the priest.

"I'm here, aren't I?"

The priest sighed. "You seem to me..." he paused, carefully choosing his next words. "To be just going through the motions."

"Oh, come on Father Sacripanti. We do this every couple weeks—I confess my sins, and you turn this into an investigation," said the man, annoyed by the priest's criticism.

"Show me you're taking this seriously."

The man took a second before he uttered in disbelief, "Father, I just confessed to you that I jerked off. I think I'm taking this pretty seriously."

"Yet you—"

"Don't you promote coming to confession?" asked the man, cutting the priest off. "But then I come so often I'm not taking it seriously? What the fuck is that?"

"I'm asking for some progress. Look, here is something for you. Jesus said, 'For my yoke is easy, and my burden is light.'"

The man rubbed his head. "The hell does that mean?"

"I have no fucking clue," said the priest, half laughing to himself.

The man was unphased. "Do you have this week's collection?"

"Yeah, here you go." The priest slid the screen away, creating a slot in the confessional, and put an envelope through to the other side.

"All right, have a good one, Father." The man stood to exit the confessional.

"Give me five Hail Mary's and—"

Right on cue, he interrupted Father Sacripanti and gave his farewell. "Go fuck yourself."

<hr />

The morning for Frankie started out like any other over the last 15 months. He woke up, showered, made his daily tally mark behind his Sophia Loren poster, then hopped in his Kaiser Manhattan and drove into town. It didn't take long for him to know the town by heart. Lazia Falls' population was a fraction of his South Philadelphia neighborhood.

His first stop was his biweekly pickup at the local church with Father Sacripanti. The priest never seemed to disappoint with getting Frankie's gears going, along with getting a hefty collection from the town. He got a kick out of the fact that the town was clueless that their favorite homily-giving priest was a corrupt piece of shit. *Yoke is easy... what the fuck does that mean?*

Afterward, he went to his usual spot for breakfast before meeting the gang at Antonio's restaurant. The stroll from his car to Lou's Diner felt oddly perfect to him. The early morning was warm with no humidity and the street was nearly empty. People tended to annoy Frankie, especially the ones here in the '50s, who seemed way too happy all the time, maybe it was just the tourists. To put it frankly, he just did not jive with this decade.

Frankie walked into the diner and sat on his usual stool. The two young girls were working, and he could see Lou in the back making eggs and home fries. Frankie had had one dealing with Lou over some gambling debts, and it had been cordial. Lou paid and gave him an omelet for the road. Frankie respected that and continued to give Lou his business. Though, that was also due to the fact the options in town were limited.

Marissa came over to Frankie with his usual black coffee. Marissa often waited on him, and despite her attractiveness, he found her quite annoying, as he often heard her running her mouth to her counterpart. Her mistakenly putting cheese in his omelet once did not help. He often wished he had some Air Pods to plug in and drown out her yapping.

The other waitress was more attractive, and he appreciated her more subtle demeanor. She had waited on him several times and had come across as personable, without asking his name or millions of other questions Frankie would not care to answer. He never made any attempts at her because he knew her father was the chief of police, and he knew better than to shit where you eat, figuratively and literally—while also staying true to where his loyalties lie.

The morning overall was going well, and he felt oddly happy. Then the roar of police sirens interrupted his tranquility. Frankie turned around, watching suspiciously through the window as the cop cars sped down the street. He looked at his watch. "No." He then double-checked the clock over the doorway of the diner. "*No.* Fuck me." He frantically got up and swiftly made his way to the diner's door. On his way out, he could hear the chatty one gloating to her friend. "Told ya!"

Frankie sprinted down the sidewalk, dodging people in his way before arriving at his car and flinging himself inside the vehicle.

In a matter of seconds, his car was speeding down the street, following the sirens.

You got to be fucking me right now.

Minutes later, Frankie was pulling into the neighborhood. Madness was ensuing as cops were keeping residents back away from the scene. Paramedics were securing the dead bodies in the street and on a nearby lawn.

"Fuck me," said Frankie, as he stopped his car on the periphery of the scene.

One of the residents was yelling. "I saw him! I saw Jesus Christ! He fell from the sky!" said Lewis, now becoming the town's evangelist. *Yeah, not quite,* thought Frankie, rolling his eyes.

Frankie started to count the bodies he could see, but the math did not add up. *Did he get—*

"Hey!" yelled a voice to Frankie's right.

He turned his head to see Dino, the chief of police, speedwalking toward his car. "Out of here! Someone rope this shit off, for fuck's sake! Lewis, will you calm down please?"

"Yeah, yeah I got it. Fuck me," said Frankie. He turned the vehicle around, retreating back into town.

Frankie stopped at one of the few streetlights on main street. Thoughts were running through his head on how he had to explain to his superiors, both here and in the future, that he had no idea what had happened or what had gone wrong this morning, when all of the sudden, a rare moment occurred. If Frankie could take a picture and show it took a group of people from the 21st century and ask what looks off? A man standing on a street corner in 1959 holding up a cell phone looking for a signal would certainly be an apparent imperfection.

Frankie parked his car and waited a minute before following the man into Lou's.

As he entered, he saw the man talking to Clara at a booth. Before he could take another step, Marissa greeted him. "You're back." Frankie turned to look at her while trying not to lose his eye on his man. "Would you like another coffee?"

"No, I'm... Actually, do you have a pen?"

Scribbling on a napkin as quickly as possible while trying to make it look legible was no easy task for someone whose teachers in Catholic school consistently hammered him for having horrendous handwriting.

After patiently waiting for Romeo to stop flirting with the waitress, Frankie saw his opportunity to slide his napkin onto the table. As he approached, Marissa cut in front of him.

Frankie took a step back and rolled his eyes at their conversation. *This clown has been called Dion and Jesus today. Looks more like Frankie Avalon to me.*

After Marissa walked away in disappointment, Frankie took his chance and dropped the napkin.

❈

In the alley, Frankie searched around and found a rusted metal pipe on the ground. It looked like something straight out of Freddy Krueger's boiler room. Frankie picked it up and hid behind the dumpster.

He waited patiently, hoping this guy was not a complete moron, for this was the only alley he could have been referring to. Then he heard footsteps come around the corner. Frankie carefully peeked over the top of the dumpster to see Jesus, Dion, or whoever the fuck he was, have his back to him. Frankie took his chance and right on cue, as the man was turning, he hit him over the head with the pipe, knocking him to the ground. A red mark appeared over the man's left eye. *That's going to hurt.*

Frankie dropped the pipe and grabbed the man by the legs and started to drag him.

"What's going on back there?"

Frankie turned to see Officer Ricci standing in the entrance to the alley. He dropped the man's legs.

"Uh, yeah, everything is fine." Frankie quickly tried to drum up a believable excuse. "My friend has a drinking problem, and I found him like this, so I'm trying to get him home. Looks like shit."

Ricci gave him a look that he was not buying what Frankie was selling. After neither of them budged, Frankie broke the stalemate and fished out some cash from his pocket and held it up with a disappointed look.

After an exchange of payment and unpleasantries, Frankie and Ricci struggled to get the man to Frankie's car, almost doing a slow waddle.

"Are you helping?" questioned Ricci as sweat started to form above his brow.

"The fuck does it look like? Watch his head," said Frankie, annoyed his effort was in question as they slowly lowered the man into the back seat.

"Jesus, you face-fuck this kid?"

"I faced-fucked your wife," responded Frankie with no hesitation.

After they finished putting the man in Frankie's backseat, Ricci held out his hand, gesturing for more.

"Oh, come on it was joke," said Frankie. Ricci did not move, and Frankie reluctantly fished out some more cash. "Bro, you're killing me." He slapped a twenty in Ricci's hand.

"That makes two of us," said Ricci with a smile. "Thanks, and tell Paulie he owes me from that thing I did with the—"

"Yeah, I got it."

Ricci did not move. A sly smile remained on his face.

"What?" asked Frankie.

"A thank-you would be nice too."

"Fuck off, will ya?"

Ricci shook his head laughing and walked away.

Frankie shut the car door and got into the driver's seat. He turned the car on, and bursting through the radio was "Venus" by Frankie Avalon. Frankie raised his eyebrows and turned to the man lying unconscious in the back seat of his car. "Yeah, definitely more Avalon."

Frankie turned up the radio, put on his sunglasses, and sped down the street singing.

Chapter 6
Jesus Is Italian

Michael slowly awoke on a green sofa in the living room of a small apartment. His head pounded, and his vision was fuzzy for a few seconds before clearing up as he sat upright.

Sitting directly across from him in a yellow chair was a man who looked to be in his early 30s, with no signs of gray in his slicked-back jet-black hair. Aiding his hair was his all-black wardrobe of a buttoned-down shirt, slacks, dress shoes, and pair of Ray-Bans hanging from the open collar of his shirt. He had brown eyes of a lighter shade and a sly grin.

"Wow, you were out. What were you dreaming? Anything good?" asked the man in black.

The man's friendliness rubbed off on Michael, despite the fact he was probably the one responsible for his current headache. Due to his calmness Michael reciprocated it, and, quite frankly, he needed a friend at the moment, or someone to at least help make sense of it all. Remembering the man's question, Michael reflected on the dream.

It was as before: empty strip club, stage, chair, Luna. But halfway through Luna's strut, and in one blink, Luna was no more. Appearing in her place was Clara in Luna's stripper garb. She strutted over, sat on top of Michael, and leaned in to kiss him. And that was all he could recall before waking up.

Before he could even say a word to the man's question... "Yeah, you always wake up at the good part. I had this dream once where this total smoke was riding me, and right when I was going to—"

"Okay, I got it," said Michael, cutting him off. He then touched the bruise on his head and winced at its tenderness.

"How is it? Bad?" asked the man.

"Bad enough to knock me out all day."

"What can I say? I'm a slugger."

Michael looked around the apartment and back over at the dream inquirer. "Who are you?"

"Someone who's stuck here just like you." He pointed to the wall behind Michael.

Michael turned and saw a poster rolled up, revealing black tally marks.

"One year, three months, and ten days. It's Frankie, by the way." He extended his hand out to Michael, who apprehensively shook it, intentionally not returning the courtesy of giving out his name.

Michael got up and casually walked over to the tally marks with Frankie never losing sight of him. Michael rolled down the poster. "Sophia Loren."

"Yeah, they don't have Pornhub here. Playboy is still relatively new. I've got the Marilyn Monroe edition in my room if you want to give that a read," said Frankie enthusiastically.

"Thanks, but no thanks." Michael sat back down across from Frankie, who didn't waste time getting the conversation going.

"So, you must have a lot of questions. Where should we begin? Why I hit you in—"

"Time travel," said Michael.

"Yes, obviously, that's how we're here."

No shit, he thought. "How?"

"That's a great question, Michael," said Frankie with a hint of sarcasm.

"How do you know my name?"

Frankie gestured to the table where Michael's things were laying. "Your license, badge. I'm not a fucking wizard."

"Yeah, I sniffed that out, thanks. So, if you don't mind sharing..." replied Michael, returning a little attitude. *This guy is a jerkoff.*

Frankie scratched his head and then used his hand to slick his hair back. "No easy way of doing this so fuck it. As I was told—which is hearsay—is that some lucky friend of ours got his hands on a prototype warp drive. This is the shit Musk and those clowns think is needed for space travel. Puncture the void of spacetime, avoiding the theory of relativity." Frankie gestured with his hands, pulling them together trying to visually help make sense. "Well, why not puncture our time? Bingo, 1959. Which, technically for me, was 1958, and it moves forward in time, sending you to my present. Now the goal was to manipulate the past to benefit the future. To be honest, who knows if this shit actually works. As far as I know, my guys from our time don't magically get cash in their pockets. Now, if you know about the evolution of the mafia, it's become more difficult because of technology. Every motherfucker now has a cell phone, cameras everywhere. We had to go into hiding. Relying more on white-collar crime and conservative actions. You know the myth if we're still around or not? Oh, we're around. But you knew that already, judging by the badge and why you're here."

"I wasn't after the mafia."

"Oh, good. 'Cause I have to say an Italian going after other Italians is just not right."

"Yeah, right," said Michael, sarcasm evident due to the tender reminder on his forehead.

"Well, you got in the way. Sometimes Italians we have to smack each other around. Did your mother give you the belt or the iron?"

"Iron?" asked Michael with surprise. The question was lost on Frankie.

"Yeah, me too. I got a brand on my ass. It's like a tramp stamp. You want to see?"

"I'll pass on the tramp stamp."

"Maybe after a couple drinks." Frankie awkwardly laughed to himself. *This guy has to lighten the fuck up.*

"So I'm guessing you're with the Testa family?"

"Yup. I work for Giuseppe Testa himself. Sent me down here through the window to help the family in the past to benefit the future right. To properly dispose of bodies if need be. To avoid situations like the one we had today."

"You're not very good at your job then."

"Thanks to you. The catch was Giuseppe didn't tell me that this was a one-way trip." He then gestured to Michael's badge. "So, Detective, when you ask how? I don't know. I have no fucking clue. I'm a soldier. They didn't tell me; they don't call or text. Which reminds me, cell phones don't get service here. So, unless you want to play solitaire or Candy Crush for the remainder of its battery life or stand on a street corner holding it up in the air like a fucking idiot then you might as well throw it in the trash. So, anyway, what did you do? You piss some guys off? Forget to pay your bookie?"

"My partner and I found some friends of yours. At a strip club, actually."

"Hide and Seek?" asked Frankie with no hesitation.

"That's the one."

"Yeah, we own a piece of that. Luna still work there?"

"I'll tell her you said hi."

"Number one rule: don't fall in love with a stripper. It doesn't end well. Trust me." Frankie's face read *mistake* all over it.

Michael chuckled to himself. *Wise words to live by.* "So obviously, a guy like you who says he's trapped is looking for a way out," said Michael, turning the conversation away from strippers and back to time travel.

"I've got to get the hell out of here. No cell phones, internet, Wi-Fi, TVs suck. I used to say there is nothing on TV when I had over a hundred channels. Try having three that are all useless. I got to get the fuck out of here. I swear my soul dies a little more every second that I'm here."

"What's stopping you?"

"The window is heavily guarded."

"Window?"

"Yeah, that's what I call it—the portal, what have you. There's a permanent one that lets you leave, but when you arrive, it's spontaneous. Example, you spawned into a neighborhood. You know, like it was fucking Call of Duty. Point is, the window here is heavily guarded by people from our future. I've been hoping I would get promoted and sneak out and shit, but I'm afraid it's never going to happen. My patience is thin as it is. So, I figure there is only one solution."

"Shoot your way out."

"Exactly. And I've been waiting for someone with the same goal and skills as me."

"Where's this window?"

"About fifteen minutes away. On a farm."

"In a barn?" asked Michael, having suspicion of its location being the same as the one in the future.

"Yup, that's the one."

"So that's the plan? Strap up?" asked Michael, unimpressed.

"Yeah, pretty much. Thing is we have three days. The guards are the lightest on delivery-day mornings, so that's the deal."

"And you've never tried before? You couldn't get anyone from around here to help you?"

"Oh, believe me, I've tried."

Frankie went on to tell Michael about Anthony, an idiot from the town who he had convinced there were large stacks of money hidden in the barn where the window was. Of course, Anthony managed to botch the whole thing by tripping in the stalks and falling into plain sight, subsequently getting gunned down.

"Just don't stress your brain into figuring out about warp drives and all that other time travel nonsense. You've just got to accept it. That's what I've learned. So stay low for the rest of the day. Tomorrow, I've got to bring you to Antonio Testa. He knows what you did on his turf. I've got you covered. You go tomorrow and ask for his forgiveness, and he'll give you a slap on the wrist for fucking with who he considers invaders on his turf and, you're set. Out of here in three days."

"Antonio Testa?"

"Yeah, Giuseppe's grandfather."

"You're working with the whole family tree."

"I know fuck me right."

"What is the Testa family doing this far outside of—" A car horned beeped outside.

Frankie stepped over to the window. "Shit. All right, I've got to go talk to Antonio on behalf of you. You'll have to hang tight so make yourself at home. There's shit in the fridge and stuff. I'll be back soon. Don't do anything stupid. We'll be out of here before you know it." Frankie ran to the door. "Hang tight." He threw open the door and exited, shutting it behind him.

◄O►

Waiting in the car outside Frankie's apartment were Frankie's crewmates, Angelo Balducci and Paulie Palumbo. Both men were in their 50s, with Angelo being in much better shape than his counterpart in the passenger seat. Angelo wore a burgundy polo shirt, and Paulie a pale-green turn-down shirt. Their dark eyes were still intact, unlike their hair, which was dominated by streaks of gray—a feature Paulie credited to his wife.

Paulie was from Philadelphia and moved out west with the Testas. Angelo was from Youngstown, Ohio and met Paulie and the Testas while bootlegging in their youth.

Angelo grew impatient in the driver seat. "What the hell is he doing in there?"

"Jerking off," Paulie replied. "Beep it again." Angelo sounded the horn just as Frankie emerged outside, swiftly walking to the car.

"I'm coming, for fuck's sake!" he yelled.

"Looks like he just dry-humped an elephant," Angelo remarked.

"He's got stamina." Not long after Paulie's praise did Frankie fling himself into the backseat. "We were—"

"Just drive," said Frankie, not letting Paulie finish his snide comment. Angelo and Paulie smirked at each other. "Jesus Christ go!"

Back inside the apartment, Michael laid down on the couch. He thought about taking his chance and hightailing it out of there, but where would he go? He was over half a century away in time, and despite his not-so-great first impression of Frankie, he knew he was his best chance of getting home.

The afternoon was dreadfully boring for Michael, who waited impatiently for Frankie to return. He tried turning on the TV, messing with the dials to unfuzzy the screen. He checked the fridge and cabinets for food, which were empty of course. "Yeah, there's shit all right."

He checked out the Sophia Loren poster, along with the Marilyn Monroe playboy on Frankie's nightstand. "Fuck this." He was going stir-crazy and decided a trip into town would not be such a bad idea. He noticed his gun was not among his belongings on the table.

He went into Frankie's bedroom and checked the dresser, tossing clothes around till he found a pistol and a wad of cash. *Italians can be predictable.* He pocketed the money and checked to see if the gun was loaded. It was.

Dino Giordano was the chief of police of the town. He had held the position for a little over a decade. It was an easy job in such a small peaceful town like Lazia Falls, but today was different, and the morning's events were what his grandmother would have called *merda*.

He sat at his office desk wearing a brown suit. He was fresh on fifty, but most people would guess him to be younger thanks to his lack of balding, and even more to his great shape, which was surprising due to how much he ate of his wife's cooking.

Standing to his left was his partner, Roy, with a notepad and pen in hand, and sitting across from him was town local, Lewis Lombardo. Both men were around his age and stature.

"So, you say you saw Jesus?" asked Dino with a wry tone.

"Chief Giordano, I swear I saw him. Jesus Christ is here! The Second Coming is here!" said Lewis emphatically.

"The Second Coming to Pennsylvania, how about that?" Dino turned to Roy.

"How about that?" Roy repeated. "Lazia Falls is so lucky."

"And enlighten me on what our Lord and Savior looked like?" asked Dino having no amusement.

"I was a bit away, but he wore dark clothes."

"Can you be more specific?"

"Uh, navy button-down shirt. Black pants. And he had dark hair and tan skin. He looked just like us."

"Well, my grandmother always said Jesus was Italian." *Rest her soul.* "How tall?"

"I would guess like five-foot ten, maybe eleven. He looked great," said Lewis, smiling.

Dino raised his eyebrows and sighed as Roy finished writing down the description of the modern-day Lord and Savior. "All right well, that will be all," said Dino as he got up and escorted Lewis out of his office. "We'll stop by if we have any other questions. Thanks for the help, and tell Bianca I said hi."

"He's back, Dino. He's back. He looked great!"

"Yeah, he's back." Lewis was too happy to catch Dino's dry humor as he closed the door behind him. He then looked over at Roy and rolled his eyes. "Wow."

Roy smiled. "Jesus looks great."

Dino shook his head. "Jesus looks great he's Italian."

Chapter 7

<u>Dream Lovers</u>

J im's garage was at the edge of town. It was the only auto repair shop available to the residents, with its own mini scrapyard in the back housing Jim's own selection of non-running cars, some in better shape than others.

Jim escorted Dino and Clara through the scrapyard as the summer sun showed no signs of restraint in the afternoon. Clara was still in her waitress uniform having to go back and work the second half of her double in an hour.

"This is all you got?" asked Dino, unimpressed as he looked at a beat-up green Chevy.

"They might not look good, but they got heart."

"Yeah, with a lot of work for me to get the heart running again. Honey, anything appeal to you?"

"No, not really," she replied unenthusiastically.

Jim was called to the front, and Dino walked up to his daughter, aware of her melancholy. "What's wrong? I can see it on your face." He'd asked the question, but he already knew the answer. "Clara, honey, we've been over this. I can't afford college for you. I can get you a used car to get you to work out of town but that's all I got."

"I know, I'm sorry. I hate to seem ungrateful."

"Trust me, honey, I get it."

"And who's going to have to break the news to mom about a car?" she asked humorously, implying it wasn't going to be her.

"I'll handle your mother, don't worry." They both smiled and he gave her a hug, doing his best to quell her disappointment. "The selection here sucks anyway," he added as they walked toward the exit gate of the yard.

"Yeah, it's shit." They both laughed at the fact she dared to curse in front of her father. "Is the car going to go better or worse than when you brought home the TV?" she asked.

"Probably worse."

———————◄O►———————

Frankie happily burst into the apartment. He'd had a productive conversation with his boss on why he was late, the situation in the neighborhood, and about Michael. He still had to explain to his liaison from the future about what had happened, but that was not Frankie's concern at the moment.

He came in holding two wrapped-up sandwiches with a smile on his face. "Yo, Michael! I got some sausage sandwiches with peppers. Fat Ralph makes—" He stopped mid-sentence as he surveyed the empty apartment. He sighed and dropped his shoulders. "Son of a bitch."

———————◄O►———————

Michael was comfortable in the warmth of the summer night. He strolled down the street, taking in the limited nightlife and lights of the town. There were people out on Saturday night, and Michael was enjoying the once-in-a-lifetime experience. Never-in-a-lifetime experience might have been the more proper verbiage.

He tried making sense of it all—the future mafia and time travel—while dealing with the current clueless mafia here in 1959.

An hour into his stroll, his stomach reminded him that it was running on empty. He saw a restaurant that reminded him of something out of *Grease* or *Happy Days* and decided to try out the establishment.

He ordered a burger and fries with a Coke and took a seat at one of the few empty tables. The place was full of teenagers and people who looked to be in their early 20s. He tried the burger, and a nod of delight led to another bite, followed by a handful of fries, and washed it down with some Coke. *Not bad, Sam. Not bad at all.*

Clara walked into the restaurant tired and hungry. She had finished working her double and wanted to treat herself to her favorite fries in town—a fact she wouldn't dare tell Lou.

She ordered at the counter, and after getting change from the cashier, she looked to her right to see Michael shoveling a handful of fries in his mouth. He looked up in his indulgent act, trying to break a smile mid-bite.

Clara's attention was turned back to the cashier as he handed over her fries. She then casually walked over to the condiment table, which was right across from where Michael was sitting. She purposely did not look at him, but out of the corner of her eye, she could see his gaze following her. *Don't say anything. Let him make the first move.*

Michael wiped his mouth with a napkin. *Think of something, don't be a pussy.* "If you missed me from earlier, you could just say so," he finally burst out.

A smirk emerged across her face, and she concealed it before turning around to face him. "The only thing I miss is the nice tip you left." She pointed to his shirt. "Hungry?"

He looked down to see a ketchup stain almost dead center on his shirt. "A little."

She grabbed a napkin off the table and sat next to him to wipe it off. "You know, I've never seen a dollar bill like the one you left."

Michael had not even thought about his money looking different. "Yeah, that was, uh... limited edition."

She looked up at his forehead. "That's a good one. How did you get it?"

"I, uh... ran into a pole."

"Some pole. Let me take a look." She rubbed her fingers on the bruise, and he instantly winced in pain. "That really is a good one. You need some ice." Before Michael could object, she was already making her way over to the counter.

She came back and sat down, ice in hand. Without warning, she forcibly pressed it against his forehead.

"Ow," relayed Michael, not a fan of the instant pain and cold sensation.

"Quit whining," she said dully. After a few seconds of awkward silence, she followed up with, "Where are you staying, stranger?"

"A friend's." Michael's lie was followed by a stern look from Clara.

"You're not a good liar. How old are you?"

"Believe it or not my birthday was yesterday. Turned twenty-eight."

"I'm guessing you're Italian, so you should know by now us Italian girls don't like being lied to. Happy birthday."

"Well, I also know you don't like the truth either. Thanks."

"I'll take truth."

"You already know the answer."

She gave him another stern look before standing up. "All right, get up. You're coming with me."

"That easy?" he joked flirtatiously, and she smiled.

"Don't make me change my mind, Michael."

"You remembered my name." He stood up, following her instructions.

"Do you remember mine?"

"Claire." He knew he was wrong as soon as he said it.

"Clara."

"Clara. Sorry. I have a little bit of a head injury that is affecting my memory if you couldn't tell."

The walk to Clara's house was filled with awkward silence, Clara telling him to keep the ice on his head, and Michael occasionally asking filler questions to pass the time. Clara made him nervous, which was a good sign he liked her. She eventually told him the story of how she convinced Marissa he was Dion.

"Who's Dion?" he asked.

"You don't know who Dion is?"

"You could say I'm a little out of touch."

"He's a singer," she replied, then started to sing "I Wonder Why."

"I guess he can't be that bad-looking of a guy." Clara rolled her eyes, smiling.

They were well into the neighborhood walk when she pointed to her house, and they turned into the driveway. "This one right here."

"Nice neighborhood."

"Used to be. Not to scare you or anything, but a neighbor was murdered down the street earlier today."

"Really?" asked Michael, acting surprised.

"Yeah, my dad's a cop. He said three other bodies were found too. It was some kind of shootout. Hard to believe in a peaceful town like this. Well, not peaceful anymore."

"Your dad's a cop?" *How about that.* "That must make you feel safe."

"Too safe. Having an Italian father who's a cop is not an ideal situation for a girl."

"Did he say if they had any suspects or if any witnesses saw anything?"

"You want to wake him up and ask?"

Michael scoffed. *Wake up an Italian father as I sneak into his house with his daughter? No thanks.*

They arrived at the front door, and Clara turned to face Michael. "You have to be real quiet inside. My mom and dad are your typical no-nonsense Italian parents, and if they knew I let a man stay the night, they would kill me." She turned around to open the door, but then turned back to face Michael. "And you too. In fact, they'd probably kill you first."

"Well, we don't want that."

———◆———

Inside the quiet darkness of the house, Clara slowly shut the door behind them. "This way," she whispered, leading Michael up the stairs.

They entered her bedroom, and she turned on the light. "Stay here. I'm going to get you a blanket."

Once in the hall, Clara shut the door behind her, concealing Michael and the light inside. Not a moment later, Marie walked out of her bedroom in her nightgown, her motherly sixth sense must have been tingling. "What are you doing up?" asked Marie in Italian.

Clara accommodated her mother's choice of language for the conversation. "I had to stay late at work."

"Do not stay up all night. Get some sleep."

"I will."

"Good night."

"Good night."

Meanwhile, in the room, Michael stood still as he heard another female's voice outside in the hall, which he suspected belonged to Clara's mother. He heard Italian being spoken, which he was not fluent in by any means, but knew that if her mother was speaking it over English, it probably was not a good sign.

After he heard the conversation dissipate, he sat on the bed and pulled out his gun from his waist which he immediately hid under the bed.

Clara came back into the room holding a blanket. She closed the door behind her. "Take this." She threw the blanket at him. "Here's a pillow," she added, throwing one off her bed onto the floor at his feet. "It's not going to be comfy, but that's the best I've got for you."

"It'll do," he said, perfectly content with the sleeping arrangements.

"I got to change into my nightgown. Turn around." She motioned with her hands. He followed her instructions as he took off his shoes. "No peeking," she added. He rolled his eyes. *I guess looking is not for free*. He turned back around after she gave the order, and she started to brush her hair.

"So where are you from?" she asked, looking in her mirror at Michael in the reflection.

"Philly."

"I've never been to the city. What do you do there?"

"I uh, do construction," he said, making something up on the fly, which he got from Henry Hill in *Goodfellas*.

"Construction? You build things?"

"Something like that."

She put down her brush, turned off the lights, and hopped into bed. "Well, good night. Hope you're not a snorer, or I'm kicking you out."

"Not as far I know. No girls have told me otherwise."

"Huh, really, haven't they?" She couldn't help but give him some attitude.

"Oh, come on, give me a break."

"This your thing? Get girls to take you home?"

"Are you jealous?" Michael immediately knew that hadn't been a wise response.

"You want me to wake up my dad?" she threatened, then gave a typical Italian-girl gospel reading. "I mean, you can do what you want."

"I'm smart enough to know that *do what you want*, doesn't mean *do what you want*," he said with a smirk.

"Wow. You actually learned something in twenty-eight years." She threw a pillow at him. He dodged it and smiled. *At least she's flirting*.

"Good night," she said.

"Good night." Michael made himself comfy on the ground with his blanket and pillow. He was silent for a few moments before speaking. "Hey."

"What?"

"Thanks for sneaking me in here."

"Yeah, well, you're welcome. Sleep tight." Clara adjusted her head on her pillow and then closed her eyes.

Michael laid in silence, and sleep found him quickly.

━━◆○◆━━

Michael woke to the sound of Clara's mother banging on the door. "Clara, wake up! We're leaving for mass soon!"

Clara quickly got up. "I'll be right down!"

Michael sat on the edge of the bed, not ready to wake up. He personally could have slept for another hour or two. There was a slight throbbing from the bruise on his head.

"Shit. I forgot about mass. Just stay here, and you can leave when we're gone. Feel free to shower. You need it." She pulled a dress out of her closet. "Don't look! I've got to change into my Sunday clothes."

"I know the drill," he said, realizing how long it had been since he showered.

⊷◉⊷

Downstairs in the kitchen, Clara's 16-year-old brother, Dominic, grabbed a piece of bread and took a bite. Marie immediately grabbed it from him. "Not before mass."

"I'm starving," he said annoyed.

Dino entered the kitchen. "You're not starving. Get your ass in the car." He then looked upstairs. "What the hell she doing?"

"She came back late last night. She works too much that girl. I wonder where she gets it?" said Marie, taking a playful shot at her husband, who shook his head.

"Clara, let's go!" he yelled.

⊷◉⊷

Back upstairs, Michael turned around as Clara finished changing. "How long you in town for?" she asked while pulling up her hair.

"A couple days I think."

She sat down on the bed next to him. "Where are you going to stay?"

"Trust me I'll be okay."

"Feel free to stop by the diner and say hi. That's where I'll be."

"I'm sure I'll see you again," he said, trying to reassure her and himself.

"I hope so."

Then the shouting returned.

"Clara, I'm not listening to your mother complain about our seats!"

"Clara, let's go!" Marie yelled up in Italian.

Clara stood and made her way to the door. "I've got to go. Bye."

"Bye," he said as she closed the door behind her.

He knelt and took his gun out from under the bed and then headed to the window where he saw Clara and her family drive away.

Chapter 8
<u>The Ball Story</u>

Michael exited the clothing store in his new '50s wardrobe—a cream-colored turn-down shirt with black dress pants. Even though his taste in wardrobe was always under attack by his female family members, he thought he'd done a great job of picking out his new attire.

He held his 21st-century clothes under his arm as he walked down the street. He passed an alley and saw a dumpster, subsequently tossing his clothes inside.

After Clara and her family had left, Michael had showered and given himself a self-guided house tour. He'd slept surprisingly well, but he still had a pit of hunger in his stomach. He'd helped himself to some bread in the kitchen and some cold cuts from the fridge. *I hope they won't mind.*

He'd exited the house from the back and carefully used a wooded tree line to exit the neighborhood. In town, he'd decided to use some of Frankie's secret stash to fund his new attire, hoping to fit in better.

Now with his shopping spree complete, he stopped at a donut shop for breakfast, ordering a powdered donut and an espresso to go along with it.

The cloudless sky let the summer sun radiate down on the town. He walked down the street eating his donut, trying not to get powdered sugar on his new shirt or pants. Multiple people smiled at him and said *hi* and *good morning*. The people here were friendlier, and they all seemed to live in the moment, which was exactly what Michael was doing.

I'll get back to Frankie's soon.

Frankie had not slept well. He'd driven around town the previous night searching for Michael. *Motherfucker.*

After an hour, he'd given up and retreated home, hoping Michael would be there and it would be an honest misunderstanding, which was not the case. He knew Michael could not have been that stupid to run away unless he hated the future that much.

Frankie woke up early the next morning and drove around the town again, hoping to find his supposed new ally. Keeping Michael on the down-low was key for Frankie. He didn't know what his future counterparts knew and was anxiously waiting his next visit from his liaison—while also hoping Michael did not do anything stupid here, or Antonio would really throw a fit. Juggling two different timelines of mobsters was no easy task.

After an hour and a half of hunting, Frankie saw his prey. Michael was casually walking down the street eating a donut. "A fucking donut." Frankie pulled his car up next to him, and Michael stopped when he saw him. "Yo!" Frankie yelled.

"Hey," said Michael casually.

"What do you mean *hey*?"

Michael held up his donut. "You want a bite?"

"Where did you get that? Luigi's? Nah, you've got to go to Nunzio's. They are much better. Never mind, just get in the fucking car."

"Listen, I'm still taking all this in, and my bullshit detector was buzzing pretty heavy so..."

"Look, enough fooling around. Just get in the car, and let's talk like gentlemen, all right?"

Officer Ricci walked by but stopped as he caught the conversation. He stopped and stood next to Michael, recognizing him from the previous morning. "Hey, how's the head? Good to see he didn't kill you." He patted Michael on the back and continued his patrol. Michael made a confused face at Ricci before turning back to Frankie.

"You're fine just get in," said Frankie, annoyed to the hilt.

Michael entered the car and sat in the passenger seat, gesturing toward Ricci. "Town's finest?"

"Yeah, well, he's got his perks. Did you have fun last night?" asked Frankie, more even-keeled now with Michael having gotten in the car.

"I did," Michael replied.

"Yeah, did ya? That's great, that's real great." Sarcasm reeked off him.

"Relax."

"Do I have to babysit you, Colombo?"

"Hey, you and your little pals are the reason I'm here in the first place. You guys killed my partner," said Michael angrily, Sam's death still fresh on his mind.

"Oh, come on. I didn't shoot lead into him."

"You're such an asshole."

"Listen, Lone Ranger. We're each other's best chance of getting out of here. I'm the one who's been stuck here for over a year, not you. You want to see your family and friends again? Or do you want to dick around here with The Mickey Mouse Club and bullet bras?"

"Bullet bras?" asked Michael.

"Yeah, they're like pointy bras. They're absolutely ridiculous. I don't know how to properly outline them." Frankie started to cup the air in front of him and pointed his fingers.

Michael had to laugh a little. "Just drive, Tonto."

"Tonto?"

"If I'm the Lone Ranger, then you're Tonto."

"Tonto, my ass."

The drive to the restaurant was less than five minutes. Frankie gave Michael the lowdown on what and what not to say to Antonio and the crew. The social club by day was nearly empty when they entered, except for Angelo and Paulie sitting at a table toward the front of the restaurant, Rocco the bartender at his post to the right of the entrance, and Antonio eating alone at a table in the back. Angelo and Paulie immediately eyed Michael. "Stay here," said Frankie. He nodded to the men in greeting as he passed them, then walked up to Antonio.

Michael watched Frankie talk to his boss before returning his gaze to Angelo and Paulie, who were still staring at him, followed by some whispering. Michael looked up to see Frankie walking back his way. "You're up," said Frankie before heading to the bar. "What's up Rocco?"

"Hey, Frankie, how we doin'?" he replied.

Michael walked past Angelo and Paulie, the two of them still eyeing him up. He then slowly approached Antonio. He looked like he was in his 70s, with the typical Southern Italian olive skin. He still had a good head of hair and looked to be fit for his age. He wore a white button-down shirt with the sleeves rolled up. He had a black napkin tucked in his shirt, probably to avoid the sauce from the pasta he was eating from staining his white shirt. First-world problem for Italian-Americans. Michael stood quietly, waiting for the boss to say something.

After a handful of awkward seconds, Antonio broke the silence. "There is nothing better than pasta for breakfast. Wouldn't you agree?"

"Sometimes I prefer Chinese food. Lo mein noodles. But yes, I agree."

"Lo mein noodles. The Orientals might have invented noodles, but we invented pasta. Don't you fucking forget it. Sit." Michael followed the instructions. "You want some?"

"No, thank you." Michael made sure to mind his manners.

"Wine?" asked Antonio.

"No, I'm okay, thanks."

"All right, suit yourself. What part of Italy is your family from?"

"Napoli," Michael said, intentionally using the city's Italian name.

"Napoli. Respectable. Second generation?"

"Third." Michael was fourth, but third sounded better, and more appropriate given the decade.

"Okay." Antonio took out a cigar. "You want one?"

"No, thank you."

"What the fuck is a matter with you? No pasta, no wine, no cigar. Jesus Christ, you a fucking priest or something?"

"Not this week."

Antonio smirked before lighting his cigar. "Now, let's talk about the fucking mess you made yesterday. I got the cops up my ass 24/7. And now they're getting ready to fuck me for something I didn't do. All because some Italian brat was shooting up some neighborhood. What the fuck is a matter with you?"

"My mother is still trying to figure that out."

"You don't work for your mother, you work for me. If you want to go do your own thing, then you're going to end up six feet under. I'm putting you under Frankie's supervision. You're lucky you got a friend like him. Lucky, I tell you. You do what he says. I take care of the cops, and you do your fucking job. Understand?" Antonio said the last word in Italian.

"Understood," said Michael in English, not trying to embarrass himself with his poor Italian-speaking skills.

"Get the fuck out of here," said Antonio, returning to his pasta.

At the bar, Angelo sat next to Frankie, eagerly sharing his newest discovery. "So, the chick starts going down on me, right. All of the sudden, she starts freaking out, I nearly popped right off my sofa."

"What the fuck are you talking about?" asked Frankie.

"Went to the doctor. My one testicle is bigger than the other. It's like a two-in-one. Left is bigger than the right. Doc said it's normal."

"I hate to break it to you, but that's not normal."

"And how do you know what's normal? You like perusing men's balls?"

"Trust me I've seen shit."

After Michael's conversation with Antonio, he headed for the door. On the way, he saw Paulie trying to get his attention. "Hey. Michael, right?"

"Yeah," said Michael, not interested in starting up a conversation, but stopping nonetheless out of respect.

"Paulie." He shook Michael's hand. "Good to meet you, buddy. You from Philly?"

"Yeah," said Michael, echoing his previous response.

"Yeah, me too. That's great yeah you know the turf. I used to have these gnocchi there that will blow your balls off."

"Giacomo's?" Michael guessed.

"Yeah, Giacomo's. Yeah see you know. I'm actually taking a trip there in a few weeks with my wife's sister. Don't ask—internal family matter. It's sort of this thing we're trying. I won't bore you with the details. It's kind of messy really, figuratively and literally to be quite honest with you. Hey, you're Italian. I got a daughter we're trying to get…" Michael shook his head mid-sentence and walked away. "Okay, yeah, no that's cool. Yeah, we're a fun family."

Frankie saw Michael rushing to the door. "I honestly thought all guys' nuts were like this," said Angelo, astounded by his testicular revelation.

"You don't want to stay for a drink?" asked Frankie. After no response, he followed Michael out the door.

Paulie walked over to sit with Angelo. "What did you say to the new guy?" Angelo asked.

"Nothing. Just welcomed him to the neighborhood."

After a few seconds of quiet, Paulie asked the question. "You tell him the ball story?"

Chapter 9
<u>Meet the Parents</u>

Frankie followed Michael outside the restaurant. "Hey slow down!" Michael stopped and turned toward Frankie with a look of annoyance. "Look the guys and I are playing some cards later. Be a nice time."

"I'll pass on jerking around with you and the Jersey Boys."

"Oh, sorry, Serpico, that you can't grace us with your presence."

Michael walked away, ignoring his companion's derogatory comment. "You want a ride somewhere?" Frankie received no response. "Fine. I'll just go fuck myself."

◄○►

Clara and the rest of the parishioners exited the church. Mass had gone well over an hour due to Father Sacripanti's twenty-plus-minute homily. Clara had nearly fallen asleep a couple times, but caught herself before drifting away, not wanting to be chastised by her mother.

Father Sacripanti was standing on top of the stairs that led down from the church's front door. Her parents shook his hand before leaving.

"Thank you so much," said her mother.

"Thank you for all you do," added her father.

"Thank you for your service to the community, Chief Giordano. You're such a vital part of our community."

Clara rolled her eyes at the priest's comments. She was about to take a step down the stairs when Michael caught her eye, standing across the street waving at her. She immediately noticed his new wardrobe with his hair looking well-kept. She waved back, and with a pep in her step, went down the stairs and made her way across the street.

"Hi," said Clara, smiling as she reached him.

"Hey. How was mass?"

"Boring. I didn't expect to see you so soon. I like the clothes."

"Thanks. Normally, my wardrobe is under attack."

"Clara." She turned her head to see her mother crossing the street, coming over to inject herself into the conversation. "Who's this?" Her mother asked with a smile as she reached the two of them.

"Mom, this is my friend, Michael."

"Hi. Nice to meet you Mrs..." Michael paused, suddenly realizing Clara had never revealed her last name. "Sorry, Clara didn't share her last name with me."

"Giordano. What part of Italy is your family from?"

"Naples. Napoli." Michael quickly corrected himself, trying to impress her.

"That is where my father is from!" said Marie with excitement, then smiling at Michael. She seemed to examine the two of them before continuing her investigation. "How long has this been going on?"

"Mom, we just met yesterday at the diner. He's visiting from out of town."

"He should come over for dinner. That would be wonderful."

"Sounds good," said Michael, intentionally responding before Clara could. "I've got plenty of—"

"Mom, can you leave us? He'll be over for dinner." Clara, did not bother hiding her irritation.

Marie gave her daughter *the look*. "Watch the attitude," she said in Italian before saying goodbye to Michael and walking away.

"You know just how to get an invitation. After dinner, we could go out. I could show you around."

"That would be great."

"Good. I'll see you later then." Clara quickly walked across the street before yelling back. "Seven! Don't be late!"

She rejoined the congregation outside and saw Marissa looking her way with a smirk on her face accompanied by a nod of approval. Clara rolled her eyes with a smile.

———◦◦◦———

Michael arrived just before seven. Clara was there to greet him in a white dress with her hair still up in a ponytail. Dino immediately met Michael as he walked in and firmly shook his hand, trying to make a good impression. He was surprised how welcoming Dino was, considering his no-nonsense demeanor. Compared to his previous experiences of meeting his Italian date's father, who had all looked like they either wanted to kill him or thought he was a loser. Probably both.

Shortly after meeting Clara's brother in the living room, dinner was ready. Marie had made gnocchi, sausage, and broccoli rabe, paired with a dry red wine, and of course some French bread on the table with olive oil at the ready.

The questions poured in, starting with where he was staying. He lied, saying his cousin's, which then led to them asking what his name was. Michael didn't know whether to lie again or say Frankie, but decided on the former, coming up with the name Jack Morrano. *More like jackass.*

"So, Michael where are you from?" asked Dino.

Michael finished his wine before responding. "Philly."

"Haven't taken a trip there in years," Marie chimed in. "What do you do for work?"

As much as he would have liked to earn some brownie points with Clara's father, he decided against it, knowing the entourage of questions that would then follow, and aware of his Henry Hill response to Clara the previous night.

"Construction," he answered.

"Labor?" Dino asked.

"Uh, contracting."

"Good money there," he commented.

Marie picked up the bottle of wine off the table. "Would you like some more?"

"Sure, thank you."

"I'll have some more," said Domonic, entering the conversation for the first time. He was instantly shot down by both his parents.

"Eat, eat," Marie emphasized in Italian to her son before pouring Michael's glass.

Michael took a sip and then decided to engage his curiosities. "Clara told me you're a cop."

"Yeah, that's right."

"She told me there was an incident down the street yesterday."

"A resident was shot in the middle of the road. Three other men were found in a nearby yard," he said grimly.

Michael acted surprised. "Wow, that's crazy."

"The three men had some interesting stuff on them. Dollar bills that looked new. We're actually trying to get the Mint in Philly to verify them." Clara looked at Michael inquisitively but continued to listen as she ate her gnocchi. "They even had these rectangular things. You press a button, and they turn on. We brought them to a local scientist, and he had no idea what he was looking at. They were like things out of a science fiction movie. Hell, the things don't even turn on anymore."

"Probably need to be charged," said Michael, quickly wishing he could retract his remark.

"Excuse me?" Dino replied.

"Nothing. Sorry." Michael sipped his wine trying to keep his mouth shut.

"We had a resident down the street who said the guy who did this was Jesus Christ," said Dino half laughing to himself.

Michael smirked at the notion that he was Jesus.

"You're kidding," said Clara.

"I'm dead serious."

"I have a hard time believing Jesus Christ would choose here as his preferred destination," Marie added.

"You never know," said Michael, still smirking.

After dinner, Clara quickly got the two of them out of the house. Dino and Marie escorted them out, and after an exchange of pleasantries and goodbyes, they shut the door behind them.

The two of them stood awkwardly on the front step for a handful of seconds before Clara spoke. "Do you like to dance?"

Chapter 10
Practice Makes Perfect

M ichael and Clara had been walking for about ten minutes before a group of Clara's friends, who were going to the dance club as well, stopped and swooped them up.

Five minutes later, Clara was dragging Michael to the middle of the crowded dance floor. The room was full of couples in their late teens and 20s dancing without a care in the world.

The dance club was in a gymnasium with wooden floors, a high ceiling, and a stage in the back. On the stage was a disc jockey with a single turntable blasting "Long Tall Sally" by Little Richard.

Clara took Michael's hands, and they started spinning around like the rest of the crowd. *This isn't like the clubs back home*, he thought. If he tried to grind up on Clara, she would probably rock him in the face. *A little early for Dirty Dancing*.

"I'm a terrible dancer," said Michael loudly, trying to get his words through the booming voice of Little Richard.

"No, you're doing fine," she said loudly as well while laughing, encouraging his obvious missteps.

"Call me Tony Manero," he said as a joke, self-aware that he was the worst dancer there.

"Who's that?" she asked.

"*Saturday Night Fever.*"

"Saturday Night what?"

"You'll get it eventually."

They continued to dance within the crowd for several more minutes, doing the hip accent, hallelujah, heel toe, and heel turn. Then the music started to slow, and after a second of silence, "Maybe" by The Chantels started to play. Everyone in the dance club started to slow dance with their partner—except for Michael and Clara, who stared at each other awkwardly. *Jesus is he going grab my waist.* She put her arms around his neck. "Like this," she said.

He then put his hands on her waist and averted her eyes as they slowly moved.

Every few steps, Clara looked up at Michael. He seemed to be looking around with that head-in-the-clouds look she'd observed on him before. *He's not even looking at me. Is he clueless?*

Eventually, he looked down right as she looked up, and their eyes locked. Their movements slowly became one, and their bodies moved closer together. *Kiss me idiot*, she thought.

Kiss her. Don't be a bitch. Michael started to lean in...

"Hey!" yelled Marissa, as she and her boyfriend Nick ran up to them.

Perfect timing, Michael thought. He had to restrain himself from rolling his eyes.

Clara released her hold on Michael and hugged Marissa. "Hi! I didn't know you were here." Her friend was oblivious to the fact that she'd clearly interrupted a moment.

Marissa looked over at Michael. "Hi, I'm Marissa."

"Dion," he replied.

She gave Clara a look. "Really?"

Marissa then introduced her boyfriend to Michael, and they shook hands. "Nick and I were just leaving. We're going to the drive-in, if you guys want to come?"

Clara looked at Michael. "You want to see a movie?"

Antonio's restaurant was empty as Frankie, Paulie, and Angelo played cards and sipped on whiskey neat. Frankie was doing well. He was up a few large on the two of them, therefore, the trash talking ensued. They just kept telling Frankie to put his money where his mouth was.

Paulie and Angelo did ask about the new guy, and Frankie made up some excuse on why he was not there. He quickly deflected the conversation back to his success on the table, though, it quickly turned into the pervasive nature that he had grown accustomed to over the past year and change.

"I told my wife I have a strict two-drink limit," said Paulie. "She asked why, and I said because I start to feel it after one drink, and after two drinks... anybody can feel it." He started cracking up as soon as he finished telling the joke, and Frankie and Angelo joined in. They each sipped their drinks before Paulie decided to turn to a more pressing matter. "No, seriously. I've been trying to get my wife to try anal, and she's not having it. She won't try it. And I explain like it's when your mother puts spinach in front of you as a kid, and it looks disgusting, so you say you don't like it, and then she's like, 'Well, how do you know you don't like it if you don't try it?'"

"Great point!" emphasized Angelo.

"You got to try it to know if you like it, right? Am I fucking crazy for thinking that?"

"Practice makes perfect!" said Angelo with continued enthusiasm.

"Exactly." Paulie was thrilled that someone shared his point of view on his sexual adventures.

"Practicing anal?" questioned Frankie, deciding to play devil's advocate.

"Sometimes, to move forward in life, you have to try things outside of your comfort zone," said Angelo, injecting his words of wisdom.

"I think I've done fine in life without getting a dick up my ass," Frankie replied.

"Fair point," said Angelo. "I mean, I've never eaten my own shit and I'm pretty sure I'm not going to like it."

Interrupting the exchange that would make their ancestors cringe, Rocco popped his head out of the kitchen. "Frankie phone!" Frankie went to answer it, leaving Paulie dissatisfied with the conversation.

"How do you know if you don't try it?"

Angelo looked at him confused. "What eat my own shit?"

Chapter 11
<u>North by</u>
<u>Northwest</u>

Michael sat next to Clara in the back of Nick's red Chevy Styeline convertible, and they pulled into the drive-in theater. The venue was packed with cars as Alfred Hitchcock's *North by Northwest* played.

They were lucky enough to get a spot dead center of the crowd with a great view of the screen, thanks to Nick cutting someone off. Marissa gave them the bird, followed by Nick and her swapping an array of colorful language with the car that was upset with them.

After they settled down from the heated exchange, and the surrounding company shooshing them and yelling to shut the fuck up, Marissa turned around in the passenger seat.

"Nick and I are going to get snacks. Do you guys want anything?" Michael and Clara both said they were fine with bellies still full of gnocchi, sausage, and accessories. "All right. Keep it classy," said Marissa before her and Nick left the two of them alone.

Clara shot Marissa a look before turning to Michael. "Sorry about her she's—"

"No, it's fine. She's great," said Michael. "I've never been to a drive-in theater before."

"They're fun," she responded. She bit her lip wondering if she should bring up what was really on her mind, in the end her curiosity ended up getting the better of her. "So, you want to tell me about the money?"

"What?" he asked, aware of what she was referring to.

"I'm not stupid. The men they found dead had the weird money too."

Michael still played dumb. "What are you talking about?"

Clara reached into her pocket. She pulled out two five-dollar bills—one old and one from Michael's tip at the diner. "See the difference? You claimed limited edition."

"It was a joke," he replied, understanding just how big of a mistake he'd made. It had never occurred to him when he tipped her that his dollar bills would be different than the ones from here. He casually tried to play it off. "Do you think I pulled it out of my ass?"

Unsurprised to Michael, she was relentless with the questions. "Why didn't you stay at your cousin's?"

"What?"

"You said at dinner you had a cousin, Jack. Why didn't you stay at his place?"

Michael had to think for a second. He was lucky that he had an excuse to not look her in the eyes and focus on the film in front of them. He was a believer in the phrase that the eyes speak, and if they were looking at her, they would be waving red flags. He continued the charade, knowing it would be futile. "You know I was locked out, and he was out with some chick, and you invited me."

"Your bruise... how—"

Michael had to cut her off, removing his gaze from the screen and focusing on her, not being able to help the subtle attitude he gave. "If you want to interrogate me we can ask your dad for a room."

Clara shot him a look of anger but kept her mouth shut, returning her focus to the screen. *Douchebag.*

Michael followed her lead. *Yeah, she's pissed.*

After a moment of stubborn silence, Michael decided it was in his best interest to apologize. "Sorry."

"Sorry," she said, reciprocating his response.

"Is that an admission of guilt?" he asked flirtatiously.

Clara smiled and gave him the finger, and they both laughed before turning their heads back to the movie. On screen, Roger Thornhill and Eve Kendall were saying goodbye at the train station. Roger and Eve were played by Cary Grant and Eva Marie Saint respectively. Thornhill and Kendall wonder when they are going to see each other again. As Thornhill took Kendall's hand before she walked away, Clara took Michael's hand. She looked just as surprised as him as they locked eyes.

Michael smiled. *Round two.*

He leaned in, and without hesitation, she did the same. They connected.

———◆○◆———

Vinny stood on a street corner smoking a cigarette. He was in his mid-30s, wearing a brown turndown shirt and khakis. He smoked his Pall Mall as he leaned against a light pole. He thought the cigarettes here were better than the ones back in the 21st century, so he always made sure to stock up.

He never got used to the trek. It always made him feel a little nauseous. But after a few minutes it would go away, and a belly full of authentic 50s Italian cuisine and a Pall Mall to top it off seemed to be his favorite form of medicine. He looked around and took a drag.

Christ, it looks like I'm working a corner.

After waiting for about ten minutes a car pulled up and stopped. The passenger window rolled down to reveal Frankie. "How much you charging?"

"If you have to ask, you can't afford it," replied Vinny.

"Fuck you," Frankie said, half laughing.

After entering the vehicle, Vinny pulled out a photo and handed it to Frankie. It was a picture of Michael.

"Who's this idiot?" Frankie asked with as much sincerity as he could fake.

"Detective Michael Morrano. You see him at all, wouldn't even know who he is? Some associates of ours botched a snag job and ended up having to grab two detectives. Philly PD reported the two who were missing. We know one is dead. The other made it down here."

"I mean, how do we know he's still in town? Could be halfway to Texas by now."

"I located him. He's watching that Hitchcock film at the drive-in. We're going to go take care of him."

"Wonderful," said Frankie, not trying to hide his sarcasm.

<hr/>

Twenty minutes later, Frankie and Vinny were crouched down at the edge of the woods looking out at the drive-in. Vinny looked through a pair of binoculars before handing them over to Frankie. "Red Chevy."

Frankie looked, and immediately spotted Michael and Clara in the back seat of the convertible. *Is that the police chief's daughter?* "That horny bastard."

"What was that?" asked Vinny.

"Nothing." Frankie quickly moved on. "What's the plan?"

Vinny pulled out a flask. "We wait."

They both sipped on bourbon, even though Frankie was more of a scotch guy. He didn't mind, though. Whiskey was whiskey to him. Vinny filled him in on the current events and pop culture of 2024 while they consistently checked on their target. Frankie enjoyed the conversation, but knew it was not going to end well for Vinny.

Back in the audience, Marissa and Nick had come back with popcorn and were sharing it with Michael and Clara. Michael was enjoying the movie, and after his intimate moment with Clara, he had a smirk on his face that he could not contain.

On screen, the bus dropped Thornhill in the middle of nowhere. Michael got an inkling this would be a good time to excuse himself. "I've got to use the restroom. I'll be back."

Vinny looked through his binoculars to see Michael heading to the restroom. "There he goes. Ready?" asked Vinny. He quicky stood up, and Frankie positioned himself behind him, taking off his belt.

"Go fuck yourself Vinny." Before he could turn around, Frankie threw his belt around Vinny's neck, hauling him backward. Vinny grabbed his gun as he struggled for air. He tried pointing it at Frankie and started pulling the trigger, making shots ring out.

Screaming, yelling, and chaos ensued throughout the drive-in. On screen, Thornhill was diving under the crop duster.

Clara looked around for Michael as people ran and cars tried to muscle their way out. Nick put the car in drive and attempted to speed away. "We have to wait for him!" she yelled. But the chaos and the heat of the moment left no time for Nick to wait.

Frankie and Vinny fell over with Vinny on top with his back against Frankie. Frankie then released the grip of his belt and tossed Vinny aside. He then whipped out his own gun and fired a few rounds into Vinny's chest.

———— ◄O►— ————

Michael ran out of the restroom trying to navigate his way through the panicking crowd. He nearly got hit by a car, but someone pulled him back out of the way.

Michael turned to see it was Frankie. "We're in trouble."

Frankie explained the situation to Michael, who thanked him for saving his life—not just from the hitman, but from the car that almost turned him into ground meat. He found it comforting that Frankie was on his side, and his trust for his accidental ally grew.

Frankie led Michael into the woods where he'd left the hitman's body. Frankie lifted Vinny by the arms as Michael held him by the legs. They carried him to Frankie's car, which was parked a quarter of a mile into the woods. They hobbled through the dark wooded area, Michael estimated that Vinny was probably one-hundred-seventy pounds. "In a span of two days, I've been called Dion and Jesus," he commented.

"Well, if you're Jesus, we're all in big trouble. And you're more of a Frankie Avalon to me than Dion."

"I don't even know who those guys are." Frankie sang, doing what Michael assumed to be his best Dion or Frankie Avalon impersonation. "I don't know lyrics to songs I don't know."

"Well, educate yourself, will ya?" Frankie immediately went back to singing.

"Just stop singing and put some muscle into it."

"Dude, I am. Fuck you," said Frankie, annoyed his effort was in question. *Second time for me in two days.*

They reached the car and carefully dropped the body so Frankie could get the trunk open. After he did, they hoisted Vinny up onto the edge and pushed him in. Frankie slammed the trunk shut and held up his arms, flexing. Michael flipped him off.

The struggle later continued as they carried Vinny down to the edge of the riverbank. The drive there had been eventful, filled with cautious driving, jokes, and a *Goodfellas* reference.

Frankie had brought a weight with him and tied it to Vinny before pushing the body into the river. They both watched in silence as the body slowly submerged into the water.

"You shall not murder. Exodus 20:13," Frankie said dully.

"You went to Catholic school?" asked Michael.

"Yeah, didn't take. Just ask him."

—◦—

Michael made his way to Clara's neighborhood and walked up the driveway to her house. Frankie had dropped him off at Antonio's, inviting him to go inside and continue playing cards. Michael refused and got a yeah, fuck you too from Frankie who let the lover boy do his thing.

Clara paced in her bedroom and looked out the window to see Michael walking up.

The front door flung open, and Clara ran to him and gave him a hug. "We left you! I'm sorry. Are you okay?"

"Looks like it."

Dino's car pulled into the driveway, and he quickly got out. "You okay?" asked Dino, concerned.

"Yeah, Dad, we're fine."

"Good. Just stay inside."

"Did you find the shooter?" she asked.

"No." He looked at Michael. "I suggest heading home," he said, before going inside.

Michael nor Clara envisioned this would be how the night would end.

"What a night, huh?" she said. They both laughed, and Michael made sure this date-night disaster would not be their last.

"Can we get a redo tomorrow night?" he asked. She agreed, and they kissed goodbye. He hoped Dino was not watching.

Clara headed inside, and Michael exited the neighborhood alone. On his way out, he passed the scene of the shootout from the day prior, reminding him of how insane the whole situation was, and the severity that people were really trying to kill him. The night had proven one thing—he did like her and hoped she liked him back. Happiness was met with sadness, and he knew this was not going to end well.

As he continued his late-night stroll, he thought of the date and the kiss, which reminded him.

It's a shame. I was really enjoying the movie.

Chapter 12
The Tramp Stamp

M ichael slept well on Frankie's couch. Frankie had bombarded Michael with F-bombs and attitude when he'd opened the door last night, but, cordially, they'd drunk a night cap together and listened to some records Frankie had collected. He'd played both Dion and Frankie Avalon for Michael before they both passed out.

Frankie had woken him up at the crack of dawn after a decent sleep on his couch, and fifteen minutes and an explanation later, they were in the car, heading to the wooded outskirts of town. Frankie had thought about questioning Michael about his love life but decided to let him enjoy his 1950s fantasy. *You're into what you're into.*

They now stood at the edge of a clearing facing each other and made sure nobody was in sight. Frankie held a polaroid camera in his hand.

"This is fucking stupid," Michael protested.

"Dude, my guys need to know you're done for."

"Just make this quick," said Michael annoyed, as he laid down on the ground.

"There you go. Just like that, Paris Hilton."

"Paris Hilton? How out of touch are you?"

"If you're telling me that Paris Hilton still isn't a smoke show, then you're lying. So put your fake blood on. And don't worry, I made more sauce for later."

Michael reached over and grabbed the tin. "Are you sure you made this runny enough?"

"Do not question my mother's recipe."

"All right where should I put it?"

"On the chest. That's where I like it," said Frankie laughing.

"You're a sick fuck."

"Tell me something I don't know."

"And I just bought this," said Michael grabbing his shirt.

"We'll get you another souvenir later."

Michael poured the sauce onto his chest, disgruntled. "Quit bitching and spread it around. Let's put some effort into it, get some production value. Now close your eyes and look dead."

———◦◦◦———

Clara woke up with a smile on her face. She ran down the stairs and out of the house, chased by the yelling of her mother who was upset that she hadn't eaten.

Clara's giant smile was accompanied by a pep in her step, as "I Wonder Why" by Dion & The Belmonts played in her head as she walked to work.

Marissa of course showed up late, eagerly wanting to know the scoop of what had happened between the love birds.

"We kissed," said Clara.

"That's it?" asked Marissa.

"*That's it*?" questioned Clara, unsure of her friend's less than enthusiastic response.

"Look, I'm going to let you in on a little secret Clara." Marissa paused.

"Okay, and?" she said, impatiently waiting.

Marissa looked around and lowered her voice. "You hear of that magazine called *Playboy*?"

"*Playboy*?" Clara laughed at the name.

"Don't laugh."

"Why? What is it?"

"It's a magazine that shows pictures of naked girls."

"What? That's disgusting."

"I know."

"How did you even hear of it?"

"Well, my mom found out my dad had one. Marilyn Monroe was on the cover. Look, my point is that men find a way to get their needs met. Whether that's through another girl or through naked women in a magazine. I wouldn't be surprised if these horny bastards are going to be watching it someday."

"Watching it?"

"Yeah, like a movie or something. Hell, I'd probably watch." Clara gave her a disgusted look. "Don't give me that Clara, please."

After Michael's photoshoot, they went home. Michael showered as Frankie washed down the trunk of his car, yelling at some of his inquisitive neighbors to mind their own business.

Frankie delivered the polaroids to his boys from the future at the farm. He could feel the pull of the window, concealed inside the barn in the back. There was no real pull, just the anticipation of the escape. Part of him wanted to just leap through now, but the guards in the back would have something to say about it.

While Frankie ran his errand Michael borrowed some clothes and decided to seek out some advice. He went to the one person in town he knew he could probably trust.

"Bless me Father for I have sinned. It's been…" Michael paused as it took him a second to remember the last time he had entered a confessional. "Ten years since my last confession."

"It's been a while," commented Father Sacripanti. "You may confess your sins."

"Well, actually Father, I'm here for some advice," said Michael casually, unsure of the response he was going to get.

"Oh, okay," said Father, happily surprised he wasn't going to get the normal onslaught of trivial sins. "Please, ask away."

"So, I'm not from around here, and I'm just visiting for a few days, and I uh…" Michael paused again before revealing his conundrum. "Kind of met this girl."

"Oh, I see," said Father eagerly.

"Yeah, and I really like her, and I just don't want to upset her, and I don't really know what to do because it's an odd situation to say the least."

"Okay, I've got some advice for you. Jesus said, 'Do not worry about tomorrow, for tomorrow will worry about itself. Each day has enough trouble of its own.'"

Michael took a moment to digest what was just said before responding. "So, what you're saying is don't worry about the outcome, just live in the moment."

"Or that all this worrying won't matter, because tomorrow, you could get hit by a car and die or fall off a cliff or something. All that time worrying will be for nothing when you could have just been enjoying yourself. Look, you're not from around here, so let me be real honest with you. Where are you from?"

"Philly."

Father made a sound of disbelief. "Let's go have a seat together." He exited the confessional, and Michael followed. They took a seat in the closest pew in front of a stained-glass window of, coincidently, St. Michael the Archangel. The summer sun radiated through the window as Father turned his back to it, looking Michael in the eyes. "Look, you seem like a good guy—handsome, probably got a good life a head of you. Clearly you've got some sort of Judeo-Christian values, but what the hell are you in here talking to me for? Like seriously man, go live your life. I don't know how hot she is, and I'm tempted to ask who it is, but who cares about some broad in this damn town? If you know what's good for you, you'll leave here for good. Dear lord, go back to the city."

Michael took a few seconds before replying, completely shocked at the priest's candidness. "I don't know whether you're the coolest or the worst priest ever."

"Probably both," he said with confidence. "I've got some extra crucifixes in the back if you want to take a souvenir with you. Grab some wine while you're at it too. If you don't drink it I will."

After Michael's head-scratching therapy session with Father Sacripanti, he linked up with Frankie, who took Michael shopping again for a new outfit. Michael picked out a baby-blue polo, and afterward, they met up with Angelo and Paulie and went on a collection spree from all the businesses and degenerates that owed them. Michael did his best to restrain Frankie from wailing on a hardware store owner. He was law enforcement after all. Trying to conduct himself in an appropriate manner was hard with this lot.

In the car, Frankie got the debate going whether Michael looked more like Dion or Frankie Avalon. Angelo and Paulie were of course split. Paulie took the former and Angelo took the latter. The conversation then turned to the Phillies, and Angelo and Paulie complained about how they sucked and how they would never see them win a World Series. Michael told them to give it twenty-one years, and Frankie shot him a disapproving look.

Paulie didn't believe it. "If you're going to talk out of your ass, at least turn around so I can understand you."

Michael and Angelo laughed while Frankie shook his head, smirking. Then Paulie decided to turn the conversation again into what seemed to be his default setting. "Young couple gets married, and the poor bastard finds out his wife can't cook."

"Must not have been Italian," said Angelo.

"First night together, the husband comes home from work, and his wife says, 'I'm sorry, I burned dinner.' So the husband says, 'That's okay honey. Let's just make love.' Second night, he comes home from work, and the wife says, 'I'm sorry. I messed up dinner again.' Husband says with a wink, 'That's okay honey. Let's just go to bed.' Third night, he comes home, and she's sitting on the radiator. He asks, 'What are you doing?' She says, 'Warming up supper.'"

They all laughed as Paulie made crude gestures with his tongue.

A few minutes later, Michael and Frankie were dropped off at the last stop. It was a deli in the heart of town. Michael stopped in front of Frankie before going in. "Go easy on this one please."

"Easy? Does a bear sh—"

"Shit in the woods? Yeah, it does."

Frankie smiled. "Good." He took a step forward then stopped and looked right back at him. "You know the horses?"

"Betting?"

"Yeah, he don't pick well." He then patted Michael on the shoulder before heading inside. Michael rolled his eyes and followed him. Inside, they saw a woman wearing a bullet bra, and they shared a good laugh; the woman was not amused.

After Frankie's tame meeting with the deli store owner/amateur horse better, he pulled Michael into an alley. "Okay, ready?"

"Ready for what?" questioned Michael.

"Ready to see the iron?"

"I guess." Michael looked around to make sure no one was watching before he obliged.

Frankie unzipped his pants and pulled them down just below his ass, and there it was, a mark shaped like an iron above his left cheek. Michael let out a gasp in surprise, and then bent over to take a closer look. Just as he leaned in, a shadow entered the alley. Michael and Frankie both turned their heads in surprise.

Standing in the alley entrance was Officer Ricci, who looked in shock at the image presented in front of him. After a second of pause, Frankie quickly pulled up his pants, and Michael tried telling Ricci it wasn't what it looked like.

Angelo and Paulie were in their car jamming to "Tequilla" by The Champs when Ricci knocked on the passenger window. Paulie rolled it down, and Ricci told them what he'd seen then walked away. Angelo shook his head and fished a 20 out of the breast pocket of his button-down shirt and handed it over to Paulie who was smiling.

When Michael and Frankie climbed into the back seat of the car, Angelo and Paulie turned around. Angelo looked annoyed, while Paulie had a smile on his face.

They did their best to explain the situation.

———— ◆ ————

Dino was on the scene at the drive-in, shaking his head. In a matter of days, the town had gone to hell. He stood away from the scene, complaining to himself as Roy approached.

"Hey, Dino, we've got tire marks back in the woods not that far from this position." Dino nodded and followed his partner.

Chapter 13
The Real Plan

A ntonio sat at his desk while sorting out the stacks of money they had collected. Paulie stood to his left and Angelo to his right, while Michael and Frankie stood opposite them. When he finished sorting out the collection, he looked up at the two stooges in front of him. "You two clowns wouldn't happen to know anything about what happened at the drive-in last night, would you?"

"No," said Frankie, and Michael echoed his response.

Antonio looked at Frankie. "Paulie and Angelo told me you left here in a hurry last night. What was that about?"

"Well, my wife said supper was all warmed up." Michael laughed along with Angelo and Paulie. Antonio, however, was not amused and shot the four of them a look. They all quickly pulled it together.

Antonio settled his gaze on Michael. "What about you? I already warned you about fucking up."

"Can't say I had the same issue."

Antonio slightly shook his head and smirked. "You two might be the dumbest motherfuckers I've ever seen. Get the fuck out of here."

They followed his wish and filed out of the office with Frankie leading the way. The two of them were heading for the entrance when Antonio called out. "Paulie, you can send my grandson in."

"Giuseppe! Get in here, kid!" Paulie yelled. Michael looked to his left to see ten-year-old Giuseppe Testa heading into his grandfather's office.

Outside, Michael turned to face Frankie as they exited the building. "That's fucking him, Frankie. That's your boss."

"Hey, hey. Before you get any crazy ideas, we're going to need to get a drink."

—◄○►—

Frankie dragged Michael to a nearby bar. The walk there had been quiet, until they had entered and ordered two drinks.

Frankie and Michael sat in a booth toward the back. Michael attempted to speak, but Frankie told him to wait till the drinks arrived, which was only a few minutes later.

They each took a sip, and then Frankie began. "Killing the kid is out of the question. Believe it or not I have standards. Not to mention we don't know what the hell would happen. This town, Lazia Falls, is where the Testas got their start, forming their own family before expanding back into the city. That's why they chose here."

"You have standards?" questioned Michael with a smile on his face.

"Fuck you." Frankie took a sip of his drink. "But it's time I be totally honest with you."

"This will be good."

Frankie put down his drink and looked Michael in the eyes. "Look, we're not just going through the window. We're going to close it behind us."

"And please enlighten me on how we're going to do that?"

"I found this physicist, Barone. Real Doc Brown type. Maybe Dr. Moreau is more appropriate. Anyway, he said that if we actually created a tear in the time continuum, then hypothetically in order to close it, you would need a thermobaric weapon with a lot of entropy. A vacuum bomb. Boom!" Frankie did what Michael assumed to be his best Barone imitation, throwing up his hands as he yelled, catching the attention of the people at the bar.

"Real nice," Michael said sarcastically.

"Yeah well, I like to put on a show. So, I paid this clown to make me one. And he did. And so, before we leave, we hit the button, on a timer, boom."

"I thought you said we don't know shit. Is it even going to work?"

"We don't. There's no guarantee it's going to work, just like there's no guarantee putting a bullet in that kid is magically going to close it, not to mention trapping us here. Hypothetically. What's the situation on multiple timelines? I don't fucking know." Frankie shook his head at the theory of time travel. "Look, I've had over a year to think everything through. I've seen that kid at least a half dozen times, and every time I wonder if I should put a fucking bullet in his skull. I mean, at the end of the day, what are you going to do? This is the path I've chosen. You're with me or against me."

"I wouldn't say I'm against you."

"I mean, I've saved your life. You at least owe me one. You don't really want to stay here, do you? You've got a whole future ahead of you."

"You sound like the priest."

"I should have warned you about him," said Frankie with a smirk.

After the drinks were finished, they left the bar and took a trip to the neighboring town to play the horses. When they came back, they stopped and got ice cream and took a stroll through the town. Two souls, out of time, wandering the streets of Lazia Falls.

They stopped at the waterfall at the heart of the town as the sun was going down and leaned against the railing of the bridge. They talked about who they knew from South Philly and realized Frankie had dated Michael's ex's cousin. Michael filled Frankie in on the ever-frustrating state of Philly sports. They then laughed at Father Sacripanti's advice.

"Yoke is easy. What the fuck does that mean?" asked Michael.

"I don't know, you tell me. You're the second coming of Christ." They both laughed at the notion he was Jesus and finished their ice cream. "Venus" by Frankie Avalon was playing in Michael's head—thanks to Frankie—as he watched the sunset.

Frankie was grinning next to him. He'd told Michael the truth, just not the whole of it.

Chapter 14

The Professor

"This is an iPhone. iPhone 15, to be exact. It's dead but—"

"Look at this thing. And it uses a battery?" asked Professor Barone, unable to hold back his excitement.

"Yeah. You can open it up." Frankie was at the professor's house, enlightening him on the future of technology. He was standing over the professor who was seated at his kitchen table. The old-style farmhouse was a mess full of copious amounts of equipment and junk. The professor grabbed a screwdriver and wedged the frame off, followed by the screen.

"Is that cobalt?" he asked.

"It certainly is. You know how many kids in Africa had to mine to get that?"

The professor continued to examine it with eyes wide and full of eagerness. "So, you're telling me that if I make you a vacuum bomb, you'll let me have this?"

"Yeah, develop it, work it. Make whatever advancements you want to make. But note that someday, and that day will come, I will find you, and I will come to collect my share of your *technical genius*." Frankie made quotation marks in the air with his fingers as he spoke the last part.

"Collect how much?" the professor asked.

"Let's go with 40%."

"40%?"

"You want me to ask for half?"

"No. I'll take that deal. I'll need a few months to get what I need and to do a test model before building the real thing, and I want fifteen grand upfront." He handed the iPhone back to Frankie.

"Well, looks like you're all out of excuses." Frankie patted him on the back and gave him some final words of encouragement. "Now get to fucking work."

----◄O►----

That night, after Frankie met with the professor, he wrote a letter addressed to himself in the future linked with instructions. While he was at it, he might as well make the most for himself in this timeline or whatever future that may be.

Chapter 15
That's Amore

R oy swiftly walked into Dino's office. "Tire marks came back," he said. "It's a Kaiser Manhattan. I went to Jim's and asked if he's familiar with any. He said one of Antonio's boys—guy by the name of Frankie Ruggiero—brought it in a few times. But get this, other than the car not being registered, I checked the records for this guy. There is none. No record of a Frankie Ruggiero anywhere. The guy is a ghost. Jim is going to let me know if he comes back. And I've got an APB out on the car."

"Ballistics came back. Two different bullets used at each scene," added Dino, who was over the whole situation.

"This guy or guys are unique," said Roy.

Dino shook his head. "Yeah, unique that's for sure."

Frankie burped as he and Michael stood around his kitchen table cleaning guns and sipping beer. "So where is this bomb?" asked Michael.

"Dr. Moreau has it. We'll pick it up before we go."

"And you know how to properly use it?"

"Of course. He showed me. Red wires go together, blue wires go together. Just like that."

"Oh, yeah, just like that. That's comforting."

"Have some faith Mr. Detective." Frankie chided.

"You can't have faith without doubt genius," said Michael, putting his philosophical knowledge on display.

"Thanks Plato."

After they laughed at each other's humor, Michael turned the conversation back to tomorrow morning's task. "So, what's tomorrow's plan of attack?"

"There is a corn field surrounding the farm. The plan is to sneak through there—hopefully unseen. Get to the barn, blast a few guys, set up the bomb, and hop through. Boom."

"That's it?" questioned Michael.

"That's it? What do you think this is, *The Italian Job*? That I've got some elaborate scheme, and we flee in Mini Coopers?"

"Something a little more precise."

"Bro, I didn't even finish high school. Once they started putting letters in math I was fucked."

"Jesus Christ."

"Yeah, well see if he's got a better plan. Cause you clearly ain't him."

"Clearly. But what if your boys hear I'm back? Then I'm fucked."

"You'll figure it out. Anyway, we don't go after law enforcement." Michael gave him a look. "Well, when you start sticking your nose where it doesn't belong, then there are consequences with something as touchy as time travel. Just keep your mouth shut, you'll be fine. If they come for you, just give me up. Tell them I went to Bora Bora."

"You don't even know where that is."

"Yeah, well, it sounds cool." Frankie and Michael both sipped their beer. Frankie eyed up Michael. "What were you doing at the drive-in?"

"Catching up on old cinema."

Frankie smirked at the answer. *Bullshit.*

⋯◇⋯

After their banter and beer, Frankie dragged Michael to a mob social club in town. The place was filled with members from other crews. Most were visiting from neighboring towns, all smoking, drinking, and playing cards. Michael and Frankie sat at a table with Paulie and Angelo. They played poker as Angelo eagerly continued the ball story. "After the shock value wears off, she makes this face like she's turned on. So she goes, 'Do you think I can fit them in my mouth?'"

Michael nearly spit out his drink, and Frankie made a face of disgust.

"Did it feel good?" asked Paulie.

"It didn't feel bad, I'll tell you that."

"Did it tickle?" Paulie followed up.

"Tickle wouldn't be my first choice."

Michael looked at the clock. "Fuck I got to go."

"What do you mean?" Frankie burst out.

"Sorry, got to go." Michael got up and speedily walked to the door.

"Go where? Just because someone else wins a hand doesn't mean you have to be a sore loser!"

Michael ignored the comment as he exited the club and sprinted down the street trying not to be late for his date.

Inside, Angelo and Paulie questioned Frankie about Michael's exodus. They gave him jabs at how the two of them had already broken up, and who was Michael's hot date? Frankie didn't laugh or answer. He sipped his drink with the most stoic look he could muster. He knew.

———◆———

After a long day of headaches and frustration, Dino was finally able to return home. He entered the kitchen as Marie was washing dishes.

"Hey," she said happily.

"Hi." The same enthusiasm was not met by her tired husband. He kissed his wife on the cheek before grabbing a beer from the fridge. "What happened to the cold cuts that were in here? Did Dom eat them?" He closed the fridge in frustration. "Where's Clara?"

"Out with Michael."

"I didn't know they were going out again."

"You may think you need to know everything."

"Isn't he leaving soon?"

"Why? You don't like him?" asked Marie, who couldn't understand why an Italian boy whose family came from the same area as hers was not universally liked.

"No, I'm just trying to remember what he said. I don't want our daughter getting too attached to him if he's going to be leaving."

"She's a smart girl."

"I didn't say she wasn't. I'm just putting my two cents out there." Dino leaned back against the counter as he sipped his beer. "Don't you think it's odd that he shows up when all this nonsense happens?"

Marie turned around at the drop of a dime. "Why would you even suggest such a thing?"

"I'm just asking."

"Well, I like him. Trust my intuition."

Dino smiled and walked up to his wife. He gave her a hug and kissed her on the cheek. "I trust you."

Less than two minutes later, Dino had the phone in his hand. "Hey, Roy. I've got two more names for you. Jack and Michael Morrano. Try those, and let me know what you find."

Clara took Michael to a nice restaurant in town. They sat at a table by the window with Michael facing the front of the restaurant. As they were perusing the menu, the front door opened, and Father Sacripanti entered the restaurant and was greeted by the hostess. Michael and he locked eyes, and Father glanced to the side to get back a better look at Michael's date. He gave Michael a nod of approval and a thumbs-up, mouthing, *Forget my advice*, before walking to his own table. Michael shook his head.

"What?" asked Clara.

"Nothing," he answered.

She turned and saw the priest. "Father is here. I don't know why, but there's always something off about him, you know? Like he's not being genuine."

"Yeah, I wonder why."

They gave the waitress their orders, and the conversation and questions ignited. He asked the question that he really wanted to know.

"You don't want to be a waitress the rest of your life, do you?"

"No, not really."

"I'm just curious—what you want to do? What your goals and aspirations are?"

"Fair question. No, I um..." She paused and smiled before answering. "I would like to be a doctor."

"A doctor," he said, surprised.

"Something wrong with that?"

"No, not at all."

"That is what I aspire to be. Money is something I don't have a lot of, so hopefully waiting tables will add up so I can go to school. But my mom just wants me to be a normal housewife. She's concerned that if I'm working, who's going to be cooking and cleaning and taking care of eventual kids?"

"God, I don't even want to think about kids."

"You don't want kids? Most people around here your age have kids and are married by now."

"Not where I'm from." Their food came. They'd both ordered veal saltimbocca and enjoyed it. Michael thought it was the best veal he had ever had.

After they both finished, Clara took the opportunity to ask her next question. "What about you, Mr. Construction? Do you like your job?"

"It's okay," he said, giving a half-honest answer regarding his fictious career path. He thought about telling her the truth, but then he'd being outing himself as a liar.

"What about your friends and family?" she followed up with.

"Well, my friends are nothing special, I can tell you that much. My family is great. You would like them. A lot of women who are a pain in my ass."

"What about the men? What's your father do?"

"My father... He passed away a little over a year ago."

"I'm sorry. I didn't mean to—"

"No, it's okay. Yeah, you know, he was a good dad. If I do have kids, I hope to be as good as him someday."

"Excuse me, sir." Michael turned to see a waiter standing there. "The gentleman in the back would like me to tell you he's taken care of your bill." The waiter pointed to the back left. On the other end of the waiter's pointed finger, seated in the back of the restaurant eating with his wife was Antonio. He raised his glass to Michael, who returned the gesture.

"Do you know who that is?" asked Clara, well aware who Antonio was.

"Unfortunately."

"Why is he paying for our dinner?" She was clearly unhappy about his presence.

"You want to ask him?"

Clara shook her head and stood. "I'm going to the bathroom."

"I'll wait for you outside."

Michael got up and walked to the exit. A woman speaking at a table he passed caught his ear.

"So, I pull down his pants, and I nearly freaked." Michael stopped and looked over at a table of three women in their 40s. The one in the middle was enlightening the group. "It was gigantic, it looked like a tennis ball." She used her hands to visualize her estimated size of what Michael hypothesized to be Angelo's testicle. "He was so embarrassed. I tried to—" She looked over at Michael and stopped mid-sentence. "Can I help you?"

Michael shook his head before walking away. *This fucking town.*

He exited the restaurant and stood outside, looking up at the stars while contemplating the past few days. The reality of the situation he was in—falling for a girl in 1959—was never going to be a wise decision. Not in the long run at least.

Interrupting his thoughts was the sound of the restaurant's front door opening. Antonio exited with his wife. "Nice night."

Michael turned his way. "Thanks for the dinner."

"Babe, why don't you go wait in the car? I'll be over in a minute." His wife headed for the vehicle while he maneuvered himself next to Michael and took out a cigar. "You know who that girl's father is right?"

"John Wayne."

Antonio smiled. "You have a sense of humor. That's good." He lit the cigar and took a few puffs to get it going. "Now let me give you some piece of advice kid. My father told me when I got into this business that you have to use two things: You have to use the brain, and you have to use the gun. Now, you've proven you can use the latter of the two. Pretty well I might add. But the first one, well..." He paused for a second and smiled. "I'll just say you're using something else. Have a good night." He patted Michael on the shoulder and walked away.

Seconds behind his departure, Clara came storming out of the restaurant.

"Clara, wait!" yelled Michael, as soon as he saw her striding off with a purpose, subsequently chasing after her.

He grabbed her arm, attempting to stop her. "Wait!"

"Don't touch me!" she yelled. She gave him a hard push to his chest. "I know exactly who you are!"

"Oh yeah? And who's that?"

"Some mob bum from the city coming here to take advantage of some innocent people."

"That's not me at all!"

"Then who? Who are you? Tell me!"

"I can't!" he said with frustration.

"Well, that's real convenient!" she said before storming off again. But this time, Michael did not chase her.

"Clara! Clara!" He paused before he let the phrase fly from his mouth. "I'm from the future!"

She stopped and made a face of confusion before turning around. "What?"

"I'm from the future."

She took a few steps forward before responding. "You're serious?"

"Yeah, unfortunately."

Clara rubbed her head and looked around in disbelief.

"I know the feeling," he added.

"You're from the future, and I'm supposed to believe that?"

Michael took a few seconds to formulate his less than elaborate response. "Yeah."

Clara looked him in the eyes with disgust. "Are you on drugs?" she blurted out.

"Does it look like I'm on drugs?" he said calmly. "I mean, I can tell you that Elvis dies on the toilet."

"What?"

"Elvis dies on the shitter, and he gets pretty fat, to be honest."

———— ◄O► ————

After their initial conversation of time travel and Elvis's ill fate calmed down, Michael led Clara over to a nearby bench in a small park where they sat down and continued the conversation. He explained everything in as much detail he could muster and make sense of. He even showed her his cell phone, which she marveled at.

"I think I need a drink," said Clara after Michael was done telling her about his odyssey.

"Yeah, I know." He looked down at the ground, a little ashamed for keeping secrets from her.

"You really are leaving?"

"Yeah."

"This isn't a sick joke?"

"Trust me, I'm not laughing."

She took a deep breath and stood up. "All right, I might be crazy, but I believe you."

"You do?"

"Am I not supposed to?"

Michael followed her lead and stood. "Any rational person wouldn't."

"Good thing I'm Italian. And you're not a good liar, so I can tell you're being honest. So, either you're right, or you're just crazy and have convinced yourself that time travel exists."

"I did have a head injury."

"Your doctor-in-training fixed that."

Michael didn't know what to say next. He could only muster the two words that he felt he should say. "I'm sorry."

"For what?"

"You know, I don't know what to say other than I wish we had more time."

"I know," she said, taking his hand in hers.

"That's why I'm sorry."

"Don't be. 'Cause I'm not." She leaned in, and they kissed.

"I don't want you to regret anything," he said.

"Not at the moment. Ask me again tomorrow."

Chapter 16
Happy Fucking Ever After

D ino sat at his kitchen table, finishing up his Frosted Flakes when the telephone rang. He got up and answered. "Hello." Roy was on the other end and informed Dino that there was no record of a Jack Morrano, and the only Michael Morrano he could find from Philadelphia was forty-seven years old. "Got it," said Dino before hanging up and rushing out of the house.

The morning was somber for Michael as he helped Frankie pack up their firearms of choice for their raid on the farm. He knew he didn't have an option. He didn't belong here, and his family—namely his mother—was certainly devastated by him missing.

Frankie, on the other hand, was upbeat and happy, which was the opposite of when Michael had walked in late last night, and some subtle remarks had been thrown out of his whiskey-stained breath.

He was stoked to be getting the hell out of 1959.

Frankie rushed them out of the apartment and aggressively drove through the town. They were on a clock, but it was excitement, not urgency that motivated him.

"Dude, do you know how many TV shows I need to get caught up on? And video games. I swear, I'm getting the new Xbox right away, and no one is going to see me for weeks."

On their way out of town, they drove by the diner. Frankie instantly regretted when he saw his companion's puppy-dog face. Not because he particularly cared, but because he foresaw the upcoming request.

"Hey, can you let me out for a second?" asked Michael.

"Stop? We're on a clock."

"Just a minute."

"What the fuck do you need a minute for?" asked Frankie, pissed they were even having this conversation.

"Frankie, please."

"Why? To see your girlfriend from the diner?"

As soon as he said it, Michael grabbed the wheel and pulled the car over onto the sidewalk.

"Hey! What the fuck?" yelled Frankie as he slammed on the brakes.

Michael exited the car and Frankie put it in park before running out in front of him to cut him off from the direction of the diner. "Oh, no you don't. I cannot believe you were this stupid. What, you couldn't keep it in your pants for three days, you fucking horny bastard?"

"Go fuck yourself!"

"Yeah, fuck me! That's right! I'm the one who's been getting fucked for over a year! And you think you need another minute with this chick? I'm the one with the wife and kid wondering when I'm coming home! They're waiting for me!" Michael made a concerned face as Frankie dug a ring out of his pocket and put it on. "How about that? I have a daughter who can probably walk and talk by now who has no clue who I am. So, get in the damn car, 'cause I'm going home!"

Michael's voice turned sympathetic. "Frankie..."

"Fuck you!" he yelled, not letting Michael finish his pity party. "Getting caught up in some 50s pussy. You want to stay? Stay! You can play house with your goody two-shoes 50s bitch. Happy fucking ever after!"

"Watch your fucking mouth!" Michael bellowed, anger creeping in.

"Oh my god! I can't believe you got hit by the thunderbolt! My fucking luck."

"Hit by the what?"

"The fucking thunderbolt, man! Like in *The Godfather* with Michael and Apollonia! The car bomb!"

"You really are an idiot."

"Hey, that shit is real, bro! My cousin Aldo married—"

"Just shut up!" shouted Michael, fed up with the conversation. "I can't take another second with you." Michael looked toward the bridge over the waterfall. "Seriously, I'm about to jump off that bridge to get away from you."

"You don't have enough balls, bitch!" said Frankie with no hesitation.

Michael's patience was at its end, and he tried to push past Frankie, who pushed back. After another effort, Frankie hit Michael where he knew it would hurt. "Fuck you and your bitch!"

Michael fully charged at Frankie, and they grappled with each other. They exchanged shots to the body before Michael took Frankie down to the ground. Michael was on top of him and punched him in the face. Frankie rolled him over and exchanged a blow to the head.

"I knew it!" yelled Marissa, who was behind the counter ready to serve some eggs over-easy. "The second you stepped in, I knew it!"

"Calm down," said Clara, unable to hide the smile.

"You got to give me the details. Obviously, it was good with a smile like that."

Clara gave her the rundown of the night, keeping the specifics to a minimum.

"Where is he? What's next?" asked Marissa.

"He's leaving."

"He's leaving? Just like that?"

"I guess." Clara's self-assurance of the situation was dwindling.

"You guess?" said Marissa as she turned her head to look out the window.

"There's more to it than that. I mean, I don't know what you want me to tell—"

"Clara! Is that... Michael?" interrupted Marissa. Clara looked out the window and ran to the door.

She sprinted across the street, dodging a car in her way. When she arrived at the two men rolling around on the ground wrestling, she took off her shoe and started beating Frankie with it.

"Get off of him!" she yelled.

Frankie rolled off and screamed in pain "Ow! Jesus, fuck!" He stood up and looked to see Clara in front of him holding her shoe. "You!" he said, his temper flaring.

Michael picked himself off the ground.

"You must be Jack," she said.

"Who?"

"Jack?" she said cautiously.

Frankie breathed heavily before looking at Michael. "Like jackoff?"

"I was going for jackass," he answered.

"Real fucking funny."

"And she knows," added Michael.

Frankie knew what he meant and huffed and puffed at the disclosure. But before he could let out more words of frustration, a car sped up and stopped next to them. Paulie and Angelo got out along with two other men, who got into Frankie's car and sped away. Paulie and Angelo grabbed Michael and Frankie.

"Get in the goddamn car," said Paulie.

"Oh, fuck me. This just keeps getting better and better," Frankie cried out in irritation.

"Now, let's go. Both of you," added Angelo.

Michael and Clara stared at each other as he was dragged away.

Frankie, before being pushed into the car, gave his shoe-hitting enemy a farewell. "Thanks for ruining everything princess. Really great job!"

Michael sat in silence, staring out the window of the car. Frankie moaned and groaned the entirety of the ride to Antonio's, drawing irritated remarks from Angelo and Paulie.

Antonio was smoking a cigar as they were escorted into his office. Michael and Frankie stopped in front of his desk.

Antonio eyed them up. "You two clowns continue to surprise me. You're like a married couple." He looked over at Angelo and Paulie, and then pointed to Michael. "You know this clown is dating the police chief's daughter?"

"Yeah, tell me about it," said Frankie.

"Don't tell me you have the hots for her too?" asked Antonio.

"Fuck no!"

"What is that supposed to mean?" asked Michael.

"If you don't think the chief's daughter is hot..." said Angelo.

"I didn't say she's not hot."

"At least he's smart enough to hit that," Angelo added.

Paulie nodded to Michael. "Good work, Mikey."

"Thanks, Paulie."

"I got good taste you know. I've got class," Frankie proclaimed.

"Class?" questioned Angelo.

"I'm a classy motherfucker I got good taste," said Frankie, doubling down.

"Classy my ass," said Paulie emphatically.

"Is everyone just going to shit on me today?" questioned Frankie, throwing his arms in the air.

"Jesus Christ, enough!" yelled Angelo. "All of you, for fuck's sake. I swear, sometimes it's like I'm running a fucking zoo." He then gave Michael and Frankie a no-nonsense look. "You two weren't at the drive-in two nights ago?"

Silence held the room, which felt like an eternity for Michael. But in reality, only a few seconds passed before Frankie mustered a response.

"Well, technically, I wasn't really."

"Oh, that's bullshit throw me under the bus," Michael immediately answered.

"Oh, let me guess—chief's daughter. Figures," commented Antonio. "But I don't give two fucks about a technicality Frankie. They fucking ID'd your car. I'm sending it to impound now. Paulie and Angelo are taking you upstate. You stay there till I say so." He then looked directly at Michael. "And you, Romeo—chief's daughter done; you're done. I'm tired of your fucking bullshit. Got it?"

Michael had no choice what to say. "Yeah, I got it," he lied.

———◆———

Dino had barged into the diner to interrogate his daughter, who was standing in front of the counter. "Where is he?" Dino demanded.

"Where's who?" asked Clara, well aware of whom her father was asking about.

"Don't play stupid with me!"

"Hi Chief Giordano," said Lewis from where he sat ten feet away on a stool.

"Not now Lewis," replied Dino before turning back to his daughter. "When you first met him, what was he wearing?"

"What?"

"Michael! When you first met him, what he was wearing?"

"I don't know. He..." She paused as she saw Michael enter the diner.

Before any of the three could speak, Lewis stood up from his stool with a smile that could have reached the heavens. "Jesus! Jesus Christ, it's you!" he bellowed.

Dino smirked as he locked eyes with Michael. He had his answer.

Michael sighed and channeled his inner Frankie. "Fuck me."

Angelo was driving with Paulie in the passenger seat, and Frankie in the back when the sirens behind them roared. All three turned around, and Frankie's response was predictable. "Fuck me."

Chapter 17

The Diamond

Michael was sitting in the interrogation room, handcuffed to the table and left alone with his thoughts. *Now you've done it, genius.*

Dino walked in and sat across from him. "Your friends didn't do much talking." Frankie, Angelo, and Paulie knew the drill. They each kept their mouths shut, except for Paulie who did ask for some coffee cake and coffee to wash it down. "Am I going to get more of the same?"

Michael did not say a word and was subsequently led by Roy to the jail cell where his compatriots were waiting for him.

"I fucking hate you," Frankie proclaimed.

"Is this going to be a circle jerk, or are we going to have to go triangle?" asked Paulie, trying to lighten the mood.

"I think, technically, it would be a square," chimed Angelo.

"No technically it be a diamond," said Frankie correcting them.

Michael sat against the wall. "Christ on a cross."

———◆———

Dino was talking with Roy in the hall when Clara quickly entered and approached her father. "Dad!" she yelled.

"Clara, you have to let me do my job," he said with frustration.

"I can explain."

"Explain what?"

Clara escorted her father outside where she explained the situation to the best of her ability. His response was about what she expected.

"Are you on drugs?" he asked.

"Dad, I'm serious."

"Do you even hear yourself?"

"What, do you think I'm making it up?"

"That boy has clearly been nothing but trouble!" he yelled, pointing inside.

"You didn't have a problem with him the other night," she quickly fired back.

"I had my suspicions."

"Then give him a polygraph."

"What?"

"That thing you said you use to see if people are lying."

"Oh, Clara, this is a waste of time."

"If I'm wrong, you can charge me rent, kick me out, not buy me a car, or give me an arranged marriage. Just trust me, please. What do you have to lose?"

Dino shook his head and let out a sigh. He looked around before moving his gaze to meet his daughter's eyes. "Arranged marriage, huh?"

———— ◆ ————

In the jail cell, the four of them figured out the diamond and sat inward facing each other.

"I don't fuck with the lights off," said Paulie with confidence.

"Really? Yeah, that's interesting," said Angelo.

"What's the rationale on that?" asked Michael.

"So I can see. So I can enjoy a nice feminine beauty."

"I prefer a dim glow, a nice dim glow. Bronzes the skin so you can see what you're doing but still has a sexy vibe," said Frankie.

"I'm a lights-off guy," said Angelo.

"Same. Lights off," agreed Michael. "You guys are overthinking it."

"Yeah, let's not turn getting your nut off into a production." Angelo added, before turning his head to the doorway. The other three did the same to see Dino standing in the doorway. He shook his head at the four of them before pointing to Michael. "You, Romeo. Up." Michael followed the instructions as Dino opened the cell.

Frankie rolled his eyes. "Figures."

Dino had Roy bring out the polygraph and hooked Michael up to it in the interrogation room. A pad that looked like something a doctor would use to test your blood pressure was wrapped around his bicep. Dino sat across from him and began administering the test after Roy left.

"All right, jackass, let's start with some easy questions. What color are your eyes?"

"Brown. Or hazel, I guess. Sometimes I would say shit green."

"I thought that was supposed to be an easy question?"

"I don't know. You tell me."

"Christ. What month is it?"

"July."

"What is your name?"

"Michael Morrano."

Dino checked the polygraph. "That's a start. Are you the Second Coming of Christ?"

"Fuck no."

Dino sneered at the response. "Yeah, I didn't think so. When is your birthday?"

"July 17th."

"What year?"

Michael paused for a second before answering. "1996."

Dino looked at the polygraph. "How about that? So, you time traveled?"

"Yes."

Dino checked again, his stern face never wavering. "What about the other men?"

"The three in the neighborhood as well. Same with the other jackass in the cell."

Dino paused, taking in the reality that the test was revealing. "Do you love my daughter?"

"I don't know. We just met."

Dino raised his eyes as he looked at the reading. "A little fuzzy on that one. Did you have sexual relations with my daughter?" Michael rolled his eyes. "Answer the question please," he said sternly.

Michael thought carefully before delivering his answer. He looked Dino dead in the eyes. "No." The polygraph started to scribble rapidly, producing a look on Dino's face that convinced Michael he might murder him. "Well, what am I supposed to say?"

"Yeah, thanks hotshot. This is great. This is just real great."

"Let's just cut this out. I'm from the future, I'm actually a detective by the way. Joke's on you. I'm here because some mob guys nearly killed me, and I ended up down here, and jackass number two and I teamed up, and we were supposed to leave earlier today, but that didn't work out, obviously."

"So fuck my daughter and leave? That's great! That's a real gentleman!"

"Look, I confessed all this last night. She knows, and we made peace with it. You're not happy with me, I get that. I fucked your daughter. I'd probably be pissed too. So if you want me to stay away from Clara, you should let me go. And guess what? You'll never see me again. I'm going back to the fucking future. You obviously aren't going to get that reference yet."

"Yeah, I'm unhappy, all right." Dino looked around, shaking his head and rubbing his forehead in disbelief. He sighed, and after seemingly shaking off his bewilderment—and more so, frustration—he looked Michael in the eyes again as he had done a minute before. "When do the Phillies win a World Series?"

"1980."

Dino checked the polygraph. "Shit."

Clara was waiting in the hallway when Dino walked out of the room. "What did he say?"

"Oh, he said plenty, trust me. Now get in the car. We're going to have a nice chat missy."

"What...?"

"In the car, now!" he said, raising his voice. He then walked down the hall as Michael stepped out of the room.

"He ambushed me," said Michael.

Clara knew what he meant. "Oh boy."

The three stooges had adjusted their diamond into a triangle, patiently waiting for Michael to return.

"A proper steak is medium rare," proclaimed Angelo.

"Both my wife and her sister order them well done," said Paulie.

"That's insane," responded Angelo.

"That's psychotic," said Frankie. "That's what serial killers order. God, I miss Outback."

"Outback? Is that a whorehouse?" asked Paulie.

Dino caught their attention from outside the cell. He gestured to Frankie. "Jackass, up."

Frankie rolled his eyes and stood up, breaking the triangle. Angelo and Paulie got up as well. "No, not you two fucks. Him!" Angelo and Paulie sat back down.

Dino escorted Frankie out the back door and into an empty parking lot. Waiting outside were Michael and Clara, who stood by Dino's car.

Frankie shook his head, smiling. "Well, what a group we have here."

Chapter 18
The Mouseketeers

D ino drove with Frankie in the passenger seat and Michael and Clara in the back. Dino's yelling ensued as soon as they left the station.

"Dad, relax!"

"Oh, don't tell me to relax!" he fired back, trying to keep his eyes on the road while looking back in the rearview to chastise his daughter.

"You're making this a way bigger deal than it is."

"Oh, just wait till your mother hears about this."

"You didn't have sex with Mom before marriage?"

"That's not the point."

"Oh, nice."

"I don't want to hear these things." He shook his head, trying not to grind his teeth. "Oh, does my daughter really just know how to pick 'em."

"You asked him," she said, not backing down.

"You did ask me," said Michael.

"I don't even want to hear one word out of your mouth back there, do you hear me?"

"Yes sir."

"Wait, you confessed to him about banging his daughter?" asked Frankie, unable to hold in his laughter.

"I was hooked up to a lie detector."

"And he tried lying too," said Dino, fuming at the situation.

"What was I supposed to say?"

Marie was sipping tea as she watched TV. She wondered where her husband and daughter were, and why they hadn't been home yet from work, which quickly got answered as the front door flew open, and the entourage entered.

Marie nearly spilled her tea. "What's going on?" she asked.

"You might think you need to know everything, but you don't," said Dino, throwing his wife's words back at her.

Marie flung herself out of her chair. "Don't you—" She quickly changed her demeanor when she noticed Michael. "Michael, how are you?"

"Hi, Mrs. Giordano. This is Jack by the way"

"Don't even," replied Frankie.

Marie turned to Clara. "Clara, what's going on?"

"Mom, I can't explain."

After a few minutes of Marie berating Clara, Dino returned from the garage with a duffel bag of guns. "All right, let's go," he said, just as Dominic came down the stairs.

"Wow! Can I come?" he asked.

"No," said both his parents, right on cue.

Dino led the way, followed by Michael and Frankie. Before Clara followed the boys out, she gave her mother one last thing. "By the way, Dad is buying me a car."

Marie lost it.

"Hey, that's not fair!" yelled Dominic.

Clara exited with her father's gaze right on her. "You're pushing it. You're really pushing it. And where is it you think you're going?"

"I'm not staying behind!"

"You're not going!" Clara ignored her father and followed Michael and Frankie in the car. "Excuse me!" She gave no response. Dino frustratingly shook his and entered the vehicle, immediately turning to face his daughter in the back.

"That's it. You're done. I hope you know you're really done this time. No car, no privileges, done."

"Great," she replied with attitude.

"And I'm inviting the Morrellis over for dinner next week, and you're going to give Gino a chance."

"Fuck no. He's horrible!"

"Don't use that kind of language with me!"

"Gino Morelli huh?" said Frankie, nudging Michael.

"Sounds like a douchebag."

"And will someone tell me where we are we going to pick up this bomb?" asked Dino.

"You know Dr. Barone?" asked Frankie.

"Barone?" Dino fired back. "Are you nuts?"

"We can trust him," assured Frankie.

"Yeah, you can trust him all right. He nearly blew up a class of fifth graders."

As they drove up to Barone's house, the front porch lights turned on, and the professor stepped out of his house.

As they exited, Barone called out, "What the hell is going on out here?"

"It's me," said Frankie.

"Frankie? You're late."

"Yeah, tell me about it."

"Is that Chief Giordano?"

"Unfortunately," he answered.

"I'm not in trouble, am I?"

After reassurance from Dino that there was no issue, Barone escorted Frankie and Michael inside where the bomb was being held.

As they walked, Frankie had a private discussion with Barone about their deal, who assured him it would be all be taken care of.

Barone then brought them to the bomb. It was a three-foot cylinder with a timer that had red and blue wires sticking out both sides and connected to the timer. Michael and Frankie carried it out to the car where Clara waited. Barone stood next to Dino as they let the two younger gentlemen do the heavy lifting.

"Sorry for that thing at the school it was—"

Dino cut Barone off. "You're fine just... stay out here. Away from civilization."

They put the bomb in the trunk of the car while being urged to be careful by Barone. They shut the trunk, and he gave one last piece of advice. "Don't blow yourselves up."

—◦—

The four of them were surrounded by farmland as they waited on the side of the road after Dino had radioed in to the station.

Michael and Clara maneuvered themselves away from Frankie and Dino. "This is it," she said.

"Yeah." It was the only word he could muster.

"Don't be disappointed. How many people can say that they met someone 65 years apart from them in time, and well, it was a good time?"

"Yeah."

"You think I'll look good in 65 years?" she asked.

"I'll let you know." They laughed. She gave him a hug, and he held her.

—◦—

Dino was not thrilled that he was stuck engaging in a conversation with Frankie, who played coy with his questions about the Antonio crew but enlightened him on his grand entrance into 1959.

"Yeah so when you go through, you just spawn into the general area. For instance, I landed in the creek."

"Then that is what must have happened to the Locatellis' roof. Someone probably crashed into it."

"Yeah, that was Vinny."

"Who's Vinny?"

"Oh, he's in the river."

Dino nodded, knowing what that meant. "Great, thanks," he said sarcastically. "You got any tips for the future?"

Frankie took a second to think. "Bet on the 1974 and 1975 Flyers."

"Who the hell are the Flyers?"

"Ready!" yelled Clara as she and Michael approached. Dino and Frankie made their way over, and Michael extended his hand to Dino, who reluctantly shook it.

Frankie stood next to Clara. "You want a hug?" he asked.

"I'll pass," she answered.

Chapter 19
<u>Red, Blue, Fuck You</u>

T he farm was mostly quiet, except for muttering between the mobster guards taking watch around the perimeter of the farm, and specifically the barn. In the silence of the night, police sirens pierced the quiet. With guns at the ready, the guards started to run to the house and driveway.

Dino and his officers exited their cars and approached the scene with Clara in the back of his car. "Stay in the car!" he yelled to his daughter.

"Dad—"

"Stay in the car!" he emphasized again.

Clara looked around and opened the glove compartment. Inside, she found a pistol. Without hesitation, she grabbed it, exited the vehicle, and ran into the stalks.

Michael and Frankie were at the back of the farm at the edge of the stalks. They'd cut through the wired fence and were waiting with the bomb next to them.

Having seen the mobster guards distracted, their plan was in motion.

"Ready? Let's go," said Frankie.

They got up and started to carry the bomb quickly to the side of the barn, which was about 20 feet from their position. They then took refuge on the back side and carefully laid down the bomb.

Frankie snuck to the edge and peeked inside, seeing two guys posted up in front of the shimmering window. He concealed himself before yelling inside. "Out of the barn! We need you out front! Let's go!" The two men ran out, and Michael and Frankie stealthily slid themselves and the bomb inside.

They laid it down a few feet from the window. Frankie grabbed the wires and spoke the magic words.

"Red, blue, fuck you." He put the wires together, and a six-minute timer started. "All right. Let's get—"

Michael and Frankie froze as the two mobster guards from before stood in the doorway with their guns drawn.

"Easy..." said Frankie.

Bang! Bang! Bang!

The two guards dropped, and Clara stood in the doorway with the gun in her hand. She ran into the barn, and Michael ran toward her. They embraced as the bomb's clock ticked down.

"Where did you learn to shoot like that?" Michael asked.

"My dad's a cop, remember?"

Michael smiled, refusing to let her go.

Frankie watched and surprised himself. *I can't believe I'm caring right now.*

"You're going to find someone great. It's just not going to be me." Clara released Michael. "Go," she said. They locked eyes as she peddled back and ran out.

"Hey. It's okay." Frankie grabbed Michael by the shoulder. "It's now or never."

Michael nodded in agreement, a saddened look evident on his face. They turned, walked, and threw themselves into the window.

———— ◆ ————

Clara emerged out of the cornfield and ran up to her dad, who rolled his eyes. "She just doesn't listen."

"Dad, pull back!"

"Didn't I say to stay in the car?"

"It's going to blow any minute!"

Dino checked his watch, realizing they were pushing the boundaries of their estimated time. "Everyone, pull back!" The cops ran back and hopped in their cars and sped away.

Clara watched from the back seat of her dad's car. Her heartbeat was faster than ever as she waited for the explosion. A minute and a half down the road, she heard the force and saw the subsequent billow of smoke. It was done.

She turned her gaze through the passenger window, staring out into the dark abyss of farmland and doing her best to fight back tears.

Dino noticed his daughter upset, and despite his frustration with the night's events, he took his daughter's hand in his.

***

Michael and Frankie teleported out of thin air and landed in the middle of the road on their stomachs. A truck coming their way slammed on the brakes.

The driver got out of the truck, yelling, "What the fuck are you doing? Get out of the damn road!"

Michael and Frankie looked at each other. Frankie started to laugh hysterically. Michael even let out a little smile.

They walked down the side of the road surrounded by fields. "You heading west?" asked Michael.

"Yeah, packing my family up and going. Look, all I'll say man, is what you did was absolutely positively incredibly fucking stupid. The universe is an unforgiving bitch."

"Yeah, thanks for reminding me. So, how will I reach you?"

"You won't. I'll send you a postcard—from Bora Bora. Does this mean we're friends?"

"Fuck me." They both laughed.

"When I said you didn't have enough balls bitch that was kind of mean."

"Just a little."

Less than an hour later, they found a bus stop and were able to catch a ride back to Philadelphia.

Frankie slept while Michael reflected on the previous few days' events.

<hr />

The doorbell to a townhome rang. Moments later, the front door opened to reveal a woman. Shock was expressed on her face.

Frankie stood on the street smiling. His wife smiled back as she held their daughter in her arms.

<hr />

Back in 1959, in the humble town of Lazia Falls, things went back to the way they'd been—except for the fact that the talk of the town was an explosion on a nearby farm. It kept Dino busy for a few weeks, which was a blessing to avoid his wife's current hostility toward him.

Angelo and Paulie were kept in their cell for about a week before Dino threw some pity at them.

Antonio made plans to move back east to Philadelphia, where his son was doing big things. He did miss Frankie, which—word on the street—was he ran away after making a deal with the police. He was even disappointed Michael had left. He had to admit, he'd liked the kid. So, in his memory, he had Rocco go to a neighboring town to pick up some lo mein noodles for him, which he enjoyed eating for breakfast.

Clara went back to the grind of working at the diner. Marissa could tell she was not the same. After a few weeks, she lightened up, and not long after, some unexpected news came her way.

———◆———

Back in the future, Michael entered his mother's house, and her and his sister immediately gave him a hug. It didn't take long for the affection to turn into a million questions, then chastisement ensued. He just had to smile; he was home.

The next day, he returned to work, which required a whole lot of explaining—and lying. His superiors wanted answers, and all he could give was half-truths and a fabricated story about being kidnapped by masked men and held in a cabin separated from Sam till he was able to escape—and a whole lot of extra sauce to put a bow on his fictional story.

When he was done being interrogated, he went to the database to find Clara Giordano.

He found her. She was dead.

Chapter 20

I Wonder Why

Michael walked up the front steps of a suburban home in the greater Philadelphia area. He rang the doorbell, and not long after did a man open the front door and greet him. "Hi. Michael?"

"Yes. Junior?"

"Yeah, come on in." He escorted Michael inside and gestured for him to sit on the couch while he grabbed coffee for them.

He came back in, handed Michael his cup, and sat across from him. "So, I have to say, I was quite curious when you left your message. Didn't know what a detective would want with my mother." He handed Michael a picture. It was a recent photo of Junior with Clara, who was much older. "I was sorry to inform you that she passed. Not long after my stepdad went, she decided to follow. Went peacefully in her sleep. But I'm sure she appreciates one of her old patients stopping by." He handed him another photo. This time, Clara was young. Didn't look a day older than when he'd last seen her, and she was holding baby Junior. "How old were you when you met her?"

"Young. I had a head injury she helped me with." Michael paused. "So, you said you had a stepdad. What about your biological father?"

"I unfortunately never met him. She always said my father had to leave before I was born. His name was Michael too. He apparently did some kind of contracting for construction and had to travel around a bit. My grandfather hated that my mother wanted to name me after him. He said he was a scumbag, but I think he was just being tough. My mom said it wasn't true. She settled on Junior, and she and my stepdad moved out to the city. She never told me details, just that he had to leave. She often said that one day he would return to see me. I just think she said that to make me not feel so bad. Yeah, still waiting." Junior sipped his coffee. "You want some pizzelles with that coffee? Let me go get them. My mother would be so embarrassed." Junior got up and left the room.

Michael was shocked as he examined the photos. "Fuck me."

The front door opened and Junior's wife and two daughters—both in their twenties—walked in.

"Hi! You must be the detective I heard about," said Junior's wife.

"Yeah," said Michael, a stunned look on his face.

Junior walked back into the room. "Michael, this is my wife, Nicole, and my two daughters, Mia and Isabella." The daughters said hi in unison.

Michael was dumbfounded for a few seconds before finding his voice. "Hey, Junior, I'm going to have to go. I've got an emergency," he said as he stood up.

"Sure, no problem. Thanks for stopping by. My mother would have appreciated it."

"Yeah. Thanks for the coffee." As he left, Junior's wife and kids said bye in unison again.

"Yeah, bye," he replied.

He closed the door behind him and stood out on the porch. He hesitated to turn back toward the door, struggling with the revelation inside that he knew deep down to be true. He rubbed his temple, coincidentally right over the eye that Frankie had bruised and that Clara had cared for. It took him a moment, but he made his decision.

He rang the doorbell again, and Junior opened the door as before. "Did you forget something, detective?"

"Would you like to grab a drink? Or if it's too early for that, some coffee?"

Junior looked back inside for a second before turning back to Michael. "I'll grab a drink." He turned toward the living room. "Honey, I'm going out!" He shut the door behind him. "There's a place just down the street if you don't mind walking. When you're outnumbered three to one, you're always looking for an excuse to get a drink."

They walked down the front steps and took a left down the sidewalk. "Hey, you seem like a good guy, and a detective. My daughters are around your age, and my wife and I are looking to set each of them up with a nice Italian boy like yourself."

"That's probably not a good idea."

"Why's that?"

Michael smirked. "Just a feeling."

Junior told funny stories about his mother as they walked. They made Michael smile, laugh, and feel nostalgic for a 65-year-old past that was just days old for him. She had given him one final gift to remember her by. A son old enough to be his dad, filling two voids that were so recently lost to him.

Christ, I guess I am technically a grandfather. Fuck me.

As Junior continued to talk, Michael looked forward, and he envisioned it. Clara standing in her room, holding their baby in her waitress outfit. She looked up at Michael and smiled.

He smiled back.

Afterword

Thank you for taking the time to read this book. As someone who has lived with this story and characters for over seven years, I really appreciate you taking the time to give it a chance. I hope you were entertained and maybe one day we will get to see this story as originally intended. If that is something you want to see, please spread the word around.

Honest reviews are one of the best tools to grabbing people's attention. If you enjoyed this book, it would be a huge help if you could leave a review on Amazon or Goodreads.

I really enjoyed writing this novella. I'm currently working on other books, and hope in the future I get to share them with you.

I wish everyone well on their future endeavors. Don't quit. Keep fighting to keep your dreams alive.